I0553116

Love in the First Degree

Hearth & Home, Volume 1

Mychael Black

Published by Arian Derwydd Books, LLC, 2023.

Robbie Sexton is heading home to north Alabama for his father's funeral. In Baltimore, he could be himself, but in Athens, Alabama, he figures he'll be back in the proverbial closet.

Then he meets Seth Ellis. Before long, he realizes maybe heading home wasn't such a bad idea. Over several months, Robbie's life winds up in a bit of a whirlwind, but there remains one constant in his life: Seth.

(This title was previously published but has been revised.)

Arian Derwydd Books, LLC
https://arianderwyddbooks.com/

Part One: July, 2006
Chapter One

"This is gonna look amazing."

"Yeah?"

Robbie Sexton caught his client's gaze in the mirror. "Oh, yeah. You still want it black? I think a bit of color would make it really pop."

Ellie didn't shrug like she normally would have. "You're the artist, hun. If you think you can enhance it with a little color, go for it." She shifted the slightest bit and pointed down at the mermaid covering her right calf. "I trust you."

Grinning, Robbie resumed inking in her latest tat: another mermaid, but this one on her right shoulder blade. He heard the faint sound of the phone ringing up at the front desk, but then the buzz of the gun drowned out everything else.

A bit later, he wiped the tat, sprayed it, and moved so Ellie could turn around and look in the mirror. Her face lit up with glee.

"It's gorgeous!"

Someone tapped the phone on Robbie's shoulder. "For you, man."

"Excuse me, honey," he said to Ellie. He took the phone and wandered back to the small storage room down the short hall. "Robbie here."

"Sweetie..."

"Mama? What's..." He didn't need to finish. He knew. He rested his head back against the wall and closed his eyes. "When?"

Mama sniffled. "Last night, in his sleep. He went peacefully, baby."

He resisted the urge to step out the back door and light up the very thing that just took his father from them. "When do you need me there?"

"Can you get here in a week?"

"Yeah. We've got things covered here well enough."

"Thank you, baby. I love you."

Robbie swallowed, nodded to himself. "Love you, too, Mama."

When he returned the phone to the front desk, the shop owner—Dale—set it on the base. Dale gave Robbie a sympathetic smile.

"Judging by your expression and her voice, I'm guessing the news isn't good."

"He's gone," Robbie said. "In his sleep."

Dale nodded and sighed. "I'm sorry, man. Anything I can do?"

"I need a week or two off. Is that doable?"

"Of course." Dale patted Robbie's shoulder. "Take all the time you need. In fact, since Ellie was your last client booked today, head home if you want."

"You sure?"

Dale smiled. "Absolutely."

"Thanks." Robbie went back to the booth where Ellie still stood, admiring her new mermaid. "Hey, honey."

She looked up and gently put her arms around his neck. "I heard," she murmured while they hugged. "I'm so sorry, Robbie."

"Thanks." Robbie stepped back a bit. He nodded. "How does she look?"

"Amazing." Ellie put her hand on the side of Robbie's face. "You gonna be okay?"

"Yeah. Heading to Alabama in a couple days for the funeral."

"Good. Drive safe."

"I will."

After he finished going over the usual aftercare instructions and gently placed the bandage over the new tat, he walked her to the front so she could pay. She handed him a tip when he opened the shop door for her.

"Thanks, honey." When he turned back to the shop, he sighed. He loved his job, but his heart was no longer in it today. "Dale, I'm taking off for the day."

Dale waved, and Robbie headed out the door.

* * *

Fuck.

Robbie shut off the truck and leaned his head back against the seat, eyes closed. They'd all known it was only a matter of time until Dad's death, but it didn't make it any easier. The prospect of going back home to Alabama held its own brand of trepidation. Down there, being gay could be a death sentence, figuratively speaking. Or, depending on the area, literally.

He got out and locked up the truck before heading upstairs to his apartment. He immediately headed for the bedroom to pack. If he planned to get out of town at a decent time, it meant leaving damn early.

He dragged the suitcase out of the closet and tossed it on the bed before opening it. Then he started going through clothes to pack. He honestly didn't have a suit, but he had nice jeans and a nice button-down. For a Southern cowboy's funeral, it would do.

As he folded clothes and put them in the suitcase, he couldn't help but think about going back home. Baltimore, while far more open than north Alabama, had begun to wear out its welcome.

Sighing, Robbie sat on the bed and raked a hand through his long hair. He looked around his sparsely-furnished bedroom. He had very little belongings, to be honest. He'd never been one for stuff. Hell, the apartment had come furnished with the basics.

He had one picture: a photo of the fields on his uncle's farm. He got up and took the picture off the wall and studied it.

"It was bound to happen eventually," he muttered as he tossed the framed photo onto the bed. He dug his cell phone out of his pocket and called his boss.

"Dale here."

"Hey, it's Robbie."

Dale chuckled softly. "I had the feeling I'd get a call from you."

Robbie stared out the window at the tiny park behind his apartment building. "Am I that transparent?"

"Nah, but I get it, man. Home is home."

"I'm sorry," Robbie said. "I would've given you more notice."

"It's cool," Dale said. "Go on home, see your mama. She needs you more than I do, Robbie. You know you got a place here should you come back up. If you look for a shop down there, just hit me up for a reference."

"Thanks, Dale. You're awesome, man."

"Just being a friend. Take care, Robbie."

"You, too."

Robbie hung up and blew out a breath. Thankfully, everything he *did* have would fit in the bed of the truck.

If anything, Mama would be ecstatic.

* * *

Cigarette caught in his lips, Robbie cradled the phone between his ear and his shoulder as he shielded the lighter from the breeze coming in through the window. Mama went on and on, relaying information he could've easily gotten directly from his uncle about a place to stay, a job, and so on. But she was Mama, and there was no stopping her. He'd told her about moving down two days ago, right after he'd called Dale. She hadn't stopped since. He tossed the disposable Bic on the coffee table and took a slow drag as quietly as possible.

"Robert Sexton! Are you smoking?"

Fuck. Obviously not quietly enough.

Letting out the smoke on a natural exhale, Robbie did the only thing he could at that moment: he lied. "No, of course not, Mama."

"Well, that's good. Burying your daddy in a few days because of those wretched things. Can't have my boys smoking now, too."

Robbie groaned quietly. "Yes, Mama. I take it Russ is going to be there."

"Now, Robert. Don't come down here expecting to make a big fuss with your brother. He's doin' good now."

What? Not mooching off of his parents, you mean?

That's what Robbie wanted to ask, but he bit his tongue. No need to get Mama all upset. She had enough going on. Robbie stubbed out his cigarette and got up from the couch. If he was going back home, he'd need to get drunk before doing it. Down there, among birth family, no one knew him. Not the *real* him, anyway.

"I promise," he said. "I won't start anything. But I still don't think it's right for him to lean on you every time he gets into a bind. I'll be there in a couple of days."

"Love you, son."

"Love you, too, Mama."

From big city to backwoods Athens, Alabama. Damn, he was insane. He had to be to move back down South. And to a *farm*, no less! He knew nothing about raising animals, baling hay, or riding a horse. Even as a kid, he spent most of his time inside, drawing and sketching. Closet or no, he knew quite a few people in his family had the sneaking suspicion that he wasn't straight. Only one of them, his cousin Danny, knew it was true; and Danny wasn't far from that sort of family himself, considering he enjoyed both sexes.

Robbie slipped his cell into his pocket and taped the last box shut. Given that he wasn't coming back, he'd decided to take his time. Either way, getting through Baltimore would be hell, no matter the hour. It also helped that the landlord was a tattoo client, which made the short notice not such a big issue.

By six in the evening, the bed of the truck was tightly packed with boxes and bags. The laptop bag went in the cab beside him. After climbing in, Robbie stared out the windshield at what had been his home for nearly three years. Then he started the truck and backed out of the parking space. Ten minutes later, he left the key with the landlord and was soon on his way out of the city.

One thing about Baltimore that he had come to realize in three years: a person had to have a healthy amount of insanity to drive in the city. And that was just Baltimore. To drive on the Beltway, one needed experience driving the autobahn in Germany. Traffic was hell, especially in the middle of rush hour. When it slowed to a standstill, Robbie did what many others had done: he turned off the truck. No doubt some jackass did something stupid way up ahead.

After what seemed like an hour, things started moving again. He put up his sketchbook and started the truck. By the time he finally made it to the Virginia state line, it was almost nine o'clock. He took the first exit with a McDonald's, grabbed some dinner, and was on his way towards Manassas.

When he hit 81 South, heading for Roanoke, an odd peace settled over him. It was dark outside, but he knew this drive like the back of his hand. He knew that if the sun was up, he would be able to see the mountains and trees surrounding him, seeming to go on forever. Fall was just a month or so away. He rolled down his window and took a deep breath as he set the cruise control to sixty.

The air outside was crisp and full of pine and earth. The mist hung low, and Robbie could smell it—clean and cool, like the fresh air of the mountains. God, how he missed that. He missed seeing nothing but trees and mountains, instead of cars and skyscrapers. He missed the sound of the wind through pine trees in the middle of winter, when he was huddled in a tent, cozy inside a sleeping bag. He longed to feel the rush of clear mountain water as he waded out into the middle of a mountain creek. Yeah. He might not love farms, but, God, he loved the mountains.

By the time he neared the outskirts of Roanoke, he was near dead at the wheel. Throwing out the idea of making it to Kingsport even, he found a quiet little hotel just outside of Roanoke. Key in hand fifteen minutes later, he parked the truck in a space right outside his room. He rummaged through the back until he found his leather jacket and then tossed it over the computer in the front seat. Making sure the doors were locked and praying to God the contents in the back would be safe under the tarp, he let himself into his room.

He locked the door, kicked off his shoes, and collapsed onto the bed. As he rolled onto his back, he tugged his cell phone out of his jeans pocket and scrolled through the phone book until he found Danny's number. Holding the phone between his ear and his right shoulder, he managed to shift and squirm until his jeans were down to his ankles, then he kicked them to the floor.

"Robbie?"

Robbie grinned. "Hey, man. You get my email?"

"Yep. Where ya at?" Danny asked.

"Just outside of Roanoke," Robbie said, absently rubbing his stomach, hand under his T-shirt. "Was hoping to make it to Knoxville, Kingsport at the least, but there was a jam on the Beltway. Got too tired to keep going."

"Cool." A few seconds passed in silence, and Robbie could hear Danny talking to someone else. "Sorry 'bout that. Russ was wondering where you were."

Robbie almost growled. "Why is he staying with you? He should be at Mama's, helping her out."

Danny sighed, and Robbie heard him moving around. A few minutes later, Danny said quietly, "Because he knows she's broke. The second thing out of his mouth when he got here was about borrowing some money."

"Goddamn it!" Robbie sat up and grumbled. "He's a free-loading son of a bitch, Danny. Why'd you let him stay?"

"He may be, Robbie," Danny said, "but he's still family. Wouldn't you let him stay with you?"

"Hell, no! I'd make the fucker get a hotel room."

"Even if you found out you're going to be an uncle?"

Robbie blinked and nearly dropped the phone. "What?"

"Kristy's pregnant. They found out a few days ago."

Robbie groaned and fell backward onto the bed. "Does Mama know?"

"Not yet. I told Russ to keep his mouth shut for now. Last thing Aunt Susan needs is to find out her twenty-year-old son is going to be a daddy."

"Yeah," Robbie muttered. "No shit." He looked at his watch and sighed. "I need to get to sleep. Gonna head out around six, so I'll get to your dad's around three in the afternoon."

"Okay. Be careful tomorrow, and we'll see you then. Need to get the kids in bed. We let them stay up late."

"See you tomorrow."

Robbie hung up and set his phone on the table beside the bed. Then he set the alarm clock for five and settled under the covers. At least the worst of the drive was over. The best part was yet to come.

Chapter Two

Five definitely came entirely too fucking early. Reaching up, Robbie pounded the table several times before he actually found the clock. He smashed the snooze button and burrowed further into the covers, reluctant to move at all. He was looking forward to seeing Mama and to the drive itself. He was *not* looking forward to seeing Russ. Ten years separated them in age, and the gap was as expansive as the Mississippi River.

At twenty years old, Russ was still a kid. He couldn't hold a job longer than two months, and he was constantly hitting others up for money. Robbie had learned the hard way not to loan Russ a dime. And now Kristy was pregnant? Robbie rolled over onto his back and stared up at the ceiling, wondering just what the hell the woman saw in Russ to begin with. After three years of dating, surely she knew what Russ was really like.

With a sigh, Robbie flung the covers off and got up. He slipped on his jeans and opened the door. For several minutes, he just stood in the doorway, eyed closed, breathing in the cool morning air of the mountains. Nothing in the world could begin to compare with it. When he opened his eyes, he felt more refreshed than he would have if he had taken a shower. Well, almost. He still needed a shower.

He rummaged through the back of the truck, feeling under the tarp for his duffel bag. When he found it, he pulled it out and went back into the room for that much-needed shower. He stripped on the way to the bathroom, tossing his clothes onto the bed beside his bag. Once the water in the shower was right, he stepped in, pulling the curtain closed. He sank against the shower wall, letting the warm water rain down on him, washing away the stress.

As he washed, other parts of him began to wake up. It had been entirely too long since he'd even jerked off. Wrapping a hand around his filling prick, Robbie closed his eyes and thought of the farmhands he knew he'd find on Mack's farm. He'd seen quite a few of them before—hard, tanned bodies glistening as they worked, smelling like sun and sweat and male. A soft groan escaped Robbie's lips, and his strokes sped up.

Jeans wrapped around muscular thighs, tight around asses made for licking and fucking. Cocks hard and leaking, just begging for a tongue to catch those sweet drops.

Before long, Robbie came, hips thrusting as he rode out his orgasm, gasping for breath. His heart thundered as he stepped under the warm spray, letting it rinse the semen from his cock and hand. Clean and sated, he turned off the water and stepped out, grabbing a towel from the bar over the toilet. He'd needed that, needed the release as much as the shower.

Back on the road, he simply enjoyed the drive, taking in the sweet air as it blew through the cab of the truck. Fuck the air conditioning. Out here, with the mountain mist so close he felt like he could touch it, Robbie was all for nature's idea of air conditioning. He breezed on down the highway, flipping through endless channels on the radio, most of them belting out country or gospel. He could handle the country—a little Garth or Reba never hurt anyone—but he could do without the gospel. He'd grown up on the stuff and was pretty much sick of it.

The drive was generally quiet, with a few stops for a drink or to pee, but then he was back on the road, actually itching to get home. No matter where he went, Alabama was always home, it seemed. Back where his family was, back with Mama—whether they knew anything about him or no. He couldn't really deny them, and despite his bitching about them on occasion, he loved them.

Then there was Dad. It was the first time Robbie had allowed himself to even think about why he was going home in the first place. Although the numbness had worn off, the ache was still there. He'd never been close to Dad, but, Lord, he certainly had never wished the man into his grave. But just like all the others, Dad had had no clue about him, no idea that his 'favorite son' was a queer, as Dad had so kindly referred to others in the past. When most others would've felt sorrow, Robbie only felt numb. He was going home to start over, to help his family, not to mourn the loss of a man he really hadn't known. He was going for Mama.

By 2:30 in the afternoon, he was turning down the old country lane that led to Four Quarters, Mack Sexton's farm. Robbie had no idea how many acres Mack really had, but he knew it was more than he'd ever seen. He'd only been on the farm a few times as a kid, and even then, he'd spent more time messing around with one of Danny's friends behind the tractor barn than anything else. God, those were the days.

"Holy shit," Robbie muttered as the farmhouse came into view.

He knew there would be a ton of people here, but, damn, he hadn't expected them all so early; maybe after the funeral, but certainly not before. Before he even made it all the way up the long driveway, he spotted Mama running across the wrap-around porch. He smiled and parked the truck, leaving plenty of room for others to get back out. As soon as he got out, Mama threw her arms around his neck, kissing his cheek and checking him over.

"My Lord! Your hair!" Mama grimaced and fussed, tugging the ponytail loose. Chestnut brown hair fell over Robbie's shoulders, and Mama looked like she was gonna pass out. "Please tell me you're goin' to get that cut."

"No." Robbie laughed, pulling back a bit to make sure there were no scissors in her hands. "I like it long, Mama."

Mama put her hands on her hips but smiled anyway. "Yes, well...we'll talk about *that* later. Right now? Let's get you inside and fed."

Robbie let her pull him across the yard and into the enormous farmhouse that was now his home. God Almighty! He hadn't been in here since...well, since he was a kid. He looked around, wondering if things were the same as they had been back then, or if he was remembering things wrong altogether. Several of the farmhands milled about inside; some eating, some drinking from cans of Coke, and others just chatting. Mack always was easy on the hired help.

"Make way, boys!" Mama shouted with a laugh as she dragged Robbie—red face and all—through the throng of bodies.

Hard bodies. Wrapped in denim so tight, it was indecent, bordering on illegal. Skin tanned to golden brown.

Oh, Lord. He could get into so much trouble right now if his left hand wasn't held by a tight, motherly grip. Fuck. He waited until they were in the kitchen, then he turned away from Mama, pretending to fiddle with something on the counter, and adjusted himself in his jeans.

"Now, Robbie, baby," Mama said, thrusting a doubled paper plate at him when he turned around. "We've got potato salad, baked beans, cornbread. Oh! And Melissa—you know, Danny's wife?—sent some heavenly sweet potato casserole."

Before Robbie could even open his mouth, Mama had a little bit of everything on his plate. He had to hold it with both hands, just waiting for the bottom to fall out. Baked beans were murder on paper plates, doubled or not. He sighed and just let Mama have her way filling his plate. Nine-tenths of the stuff he probably wouldn't even touch.

At least there was fried chicken. Now *that* had his mouth watering...kind of like that tall, golden-skinned sun god staring at him from across the expanse of the den. Dear God. Robbie would have dropped everything just for a single taste of that sun-kissed body.

"Robert Sexton!"

Robbie shook his head quickly, warmth creeping up his neck and cheeks when he realized the sun god in a cowboy hat was laughing at him. "What?" Robbie asked, turning back to Mama.

"I was askin' you what you wanted to drink, baby," Mama said. She leaned to the side and peered into the den. Robbie was actually grateful the cowboy had moved. When Mama looked back to him, her face wrinkled with concern. "You feeling okay, Robert? You're lookin' feverish."

"I'm fine," Robbie choked out, desperate to will away the terminal hard-on trying to make itself known. "Just tired from the drive, I guess."

Mama seemed to take that well enough. "Well, you just eat and relax, baby. There's plenty of room in the den if you push some of the boys out of the way."

Oh. No way in hell was he going to eat inside. Not food at any rate.

"Thanks, Mama," Robbie said, "but I think I'll find a spot outside. Less crowded."

Mama nodded and handed him a cold can of Coke.

Plate balanced precariously on one palm and a Coke in the other hand, Robbie slipped out the screen door in the kitchen and into the backyard. He found a nice quiet spot against the trunk of an ancient-looking oak and settled back as he ate his lunch. He could hear kids screaming and laughing around the front, and a few minutes later, he was fending off four sticky hands. His attackers gave him just enough time to set his plate and Coke down, and then they were on him full-force, small bodies taking him down in a pile of limbs and giggles. And fur?

"Oh, man!" Robbie swatted the dog away, getting a tongue bath from the elbow up for his efforts. When he looked over, two pairs of crystal blues eyes met his own: Julia and Taylor—Danny and Melissa's rugrats. Robbie was more an uncle than a cousin to them.

"When'd ya get in?" eleven-year-old Taylor asked, dropping down by Robbie's head to pet Rocks, their Lab who thought he was a Chihuahua.

"About twenty minutes ago." Robbie sat up and dragged Taylor's five-year-old sister Julia into a hug. "Where's your daddy?"

"Still inside," Taylor said as he stole a bite off a chicken leg. "Tryin' to keep Mama off the cowboys."

Robbie bit his tongue as another shadow darkened the immediate area. "Why don't you two go get something to eat?" As soon as the kids left, Danny sat down beside him. "Scopin' out the cowboys, huh?"

Danny chuckled. "Can ya blame me?"

Thinking about the sun god in a Stetson, Robbie shook his head. "Hell, no."

"You see the cowboy in the black hat?" Danny grinned at him.

Robbie laughed. "You fuckin' kidding? I nearly drooled in front of Mama."

"He's family," Danny said. There was more than a hint in his tone. Robbie just stared at him. "He is! Met him 'bout three weeks ago in Huntsville. They got a new bar over there. Met him and kinda chummed it up for a while. He was new in town, from Houston, and lookin' for work. Told him about Dad's farm, and, well, here he is. Oh, and he's single."

Robbie groaned. "How the hell am I supposed to work around the man and *not* stare?"

Danny smirked and clapped a hand on Robbie's shoulder. "That's your problem, cuz. I might've mentioned you a few times to him."

Robbie rolled his eyes and fell backward onto the ground. "This should be interesting."

Chapter Three

"Wow. Very nice. You an artist?"

The sexy drawl pulled Robbie's attention from the sketchbook on his lap to the tall, tanned body standing in front of him. If he looked straight ahead, his line of sight was dead level with the man's crotch. Even through a layer of faded denim, it was obvious the man had plenty to offer. Gaze continuing upward, Robbie drank in the sweat-slick skin, stretched taut over chiseled muscles and tanned to soft gold. A light dusting of pale brown hair—bleached gold by the sun—began at the man's chest and drew a path down his sun-kissed torso, only to disappear beneath his jeans.

His shoulders were broad, and the sleeves of his open blue plaid shirt were rolled up, tight around hard biceps. A black cowboy hat sat on his head, cocked forward just enough to hide his face. Then the man tipped the hat back, taking Robbie's breath away. Eyes greener than the new spring grass reflected the man's easy smile. The slightest hint of a five o'clock shadow gave him a ruggedly sexy look. Not that he needed the help.

"Name's Seth Ellis," the sun god said, extending a hand downward.

Regaining his composure, Robbie stood and brushed the grass off of his right hand before shaking Seth's. "Robbie Sexton."

"I'm really sorry about your dad."

"Thanks," Robbie said. As Seth released his hand, Robbie noticed it was done with a bit of hesitation. Now that was promising. "I'm gonna grab a beer. You wanna join me?"

"Sure."

Robbie snuck around the porch and into the front yard, snagging two beer bottles from one of the big coolers and making it away without being seen. Hell, yes! The day was looking up! He returned to Seth and handed him one of the bottles.

"Follow me," he said. "I know some of the best places around here where a man can find some peace."

"Of what?" Seth chuckled before taking a long drink.

Robbie glanced over at him. "If the right person's offering..." He left the rest unsaid, waiting to see if Seth took the bait.

A smile played across Seth's lips just before they oh-so-slowly wrapped around the mouth of the beer bottle. "So," Seth said after his sip, "*is* he offering?" He flashed Robbie a wicked grin from behind the bottle, followed by a quick wink.

Robbie's throat went dry as cotton as he stared at Seth, or rather Seth's tongue as it did obscene things to the beer bottle. What the hell had Danny been telling the man?

Clearing his throat, Robbie remembered how to do something other than stare. "I'm guessing you've spoken to my cousin Danny."

Seth grinned. "You could say that."

Robbie licked his lips. If anything, life wouldn't be boring here now. "This way," he said quickly. He forced himself to walk when he wanted to run.

Just as they rounded the corner of the combine barn, a strong hand gripped his arm. Within seconds, Robbie was captive, body caught between the hard metal building and an equally hard cowboy. Hips rocking, Seth ground against him, tongue pushing into Robbie's mouth without any hesitation. The cowboy tasted like beer and sun and male, blazing hot, breath almost scorching as the kiss moved from Robbie's mouth to his throat.

"Oh, fuck," Robbie breathed. His head swam as long fingers found the button of his jeans, popping them open. Then those fingers were inside, slipping into his underwear, tips brushing the head of his prick. Robbie gasped and held on, arms draped over Seth's shoulders.

"So hot," Seth murmured, moving back up to take Robbie's mouth in another searing kiss.

God, this man was unbelievable. Too fucking good to be real, Robbie thought. Too fucking...oh, God.

Thumb stroking over his slit, Seth had Robbie melting against him. Don't stop, Robbie tried to say, but nothing came out. His heart pounded as he thrust into the fist closing around his cock. Robbie's legs shook, and heat slid up his spine as Seth almost growled into his mouth. Feeding the cowboy moans and gasps, Robbie jerked hard, heat spilling over Seth's fingers. He was too fucking dazed to even feel embarrassed.

As his brain started to clear, Robbie was acutely aware of hardness pressing against his thigh. Seth stared down at him, green eyes full of lust-fueled fire, pink tongue sliding across kiss-swollen lips. When he looked down, he saw the outline of the cowboy's cock through his jeans. If he looked hard enough, Robbie imagined he could see that thick length of steel throbbing. He wanted to taste that, to drink in the salty-sweet drops. He turned Seth quickly and dropped to his knees, fingers working quickly to unleash the hard-on waiting just inside the denim.

As soon as he peeled Seth's jeans open, Robbie's mouth began to water. Beneath a thin layer of white cotton, wetness pooled near the top, soaking the material around the tip of Seth's prick. Robbie leaned forward and breathed deep, shivering as the smell of earth, hay, sun, and sweat washed over him.

Oh, yes. Oh, hell, yes.

Eyes rolling up to meet a crystal green gaze, Robbie nibbled at the wet spot, his spit mixing with the sweet pre-come. Seth's eyes rolled slowly back in his head, and his fingers slid through Robbie's hair, caught in the ponytail, and tugged it loose. Robbie shuddered as those long fingers stroked his hair, his neck, his scalp. Then he returned his attention to the delicious sight before him. Hooking his fingers in the waistband of Seth's underwear, Robbie tugged them down, getting his first look at a cock larger than he had originally expected.

Gentle pressure to the back of his head brought him closer, and Robbie slid his tongue from the base of Seth's cock to the tip, stopping just long enough to tongue the slit before sliding back down. Seth groaned softly and massaged his hair, hips rocking ever-so-slightly. Wrapping a hand around the thick shaft, Robbie planted a sucking kiss just to the head, taking care to nibble lightly on the foreskin. A slow shudder from the cowboy was his sweet reward. Robbie grinned and sucked half of Seth's length down his throat.

Seth's fingers tightened in his hair, tugging him close. "Don't stop, Robbie."

Robbie shook his head quickly and used his free hand to pull Seth's jeans down just a bit more. He cupped the cowboy's heavy balls, rolling them in his palm, pressing with his fingertips to the small spot just behind them. A low sound escaped Seth, and his hips jerked forward, cocking jumping in Robbie's mouth. Pulling back to the tip again, Robbie scraped his teeth lightly along the shaft. Seth gasped and grunted, then thrust back in. Robbie swallowed quickly, stroking Seth's gland from the outside, drinking in as much of the cowboy's release as he could. When Seth slumped back against the wall, his softening cock slipped from Robbie's mouth. Robbie licked his lips and stood, pushing his tongue into Seth's mouth. Seth groaned and cupped the back of his head, deepening the kiss with a growl.

The need for air was the only thing that broke the kiss. Robbie leaned against Seth's chest, shivering slightly when the cowboy's long fingers traced his spine.

"I don't think I've ever done that," Robbie muttered.

"Sucked a guy off?"

Robbie laughed. "That quickly after meeting, I mean." He glanced up. "Something tells me my cousin is playing matchmaker."

Seth shrugged. "He might've shown me a pic...or four."

Robbie rolled his eyes. "That explains a lot."

"We need to get back to the others at some point," Seth said. "Really don't need anyone to come hunting us down."

Robbie nodded reluctantly. "Yeah, I know."

"Don't suppose you live anywhere 'round here?"

Stepping back just enough for Seth to get his jeans back up, Robbie ran his fingers through his hair. "Well, yeah, kinda do now. Was up in Baltimore for about three years, but I'm moving back down here."

"What did you do up there?"

"Tattoo artist," Robbie said.

Seth buttoned his jeans. "Really?"

Robbie lifted his T-shirt and grinned as the cowboy's eyes went wide. "Yup. Obviously, I didn't ink these, but I designed them."

"Wow," Seth whispered in awe. He traced the outline of the dragon's blue scaly body as it slithered diagonally across Robbie's chest. "You design this one?"

"And this one," Robbie said, pulling off his shirt and turning around. The Celtic cross would be a shocker to Mama if she ever caught sight of it. "Always wanted a backpiece. Designed this one about two years ago and got it done." He shivered as Seth's hand smoothed over his back, then down to trace the seam of his jeans, following it along the crease of his ass. Hot breath caressed his shoulder, the back of his neck, as Seth moved his hair away.

"Very nice," Seth whispered. The light dance of fingers down his ass made Robbie wonder if Seth was still talking about tats. Probably not. "Got anymore?" Robbie nodded. "Where?"

Turning around, Robbie just grinned. "Guess you'll just have to find out, won't you, Cowboy?"

Seth jerked him close to that heated, hard body. "Yeah. Guess so."

They made their way back to the house, keeping a safe distance apart as they chatted idly. No need in stirring shit up. Then they rounded the house and came upon the one person

Robbie did *not* want to see. He stopped dead in his tracks and directed an icy glare at the head of disheveled brown hair only a few feet in front of them.

Seth nudged his arm with an elbow. "What's up?"

Robbie shook his head and turned away before Russ could figure out that he was being stared at. As soon as he and Seth were around the side of the house, Robbie slammed his fist into the nearest pear tree trunk.

"Son of a bitch!" He growled and spun around, sinking to the ground along the trunk. Seth plopped down a couple of feet away from him. "He's my brother—Russ. Goddamned freeloading, worthless piece of shit."

"Take it you two don't get along well," Seth said.

"Not in the least. He's only ten years younger, but, damn, the gap between us feels like fuckin' decades."

Robbie shifted slightly and tugged a crushed pack of cigarettes out of his jeans pocket. Before he could get his lighter out, however, Seth leaned forward, lighter in hand.

"Thanks," Robbie said, taking a slow, much-needed pull from the Marlboro Red. He met a wry, almost sympathetic smile as he blew the smoke out. "What?"

"How old *are* you anyway?" Seth asked as he lit up his own cigarette.

"Thirty." Robbie took another drag and sighed. "You?"

"Thirty-four." The grin that followed was part relief, part devilish. Taking a quick glance around, Seth leaned forward and gave him a quick but thorough kiss.

"What was that for?"

The cowboy shrugged. "Just because. You taste good."

Robbie swallowed hard and cursed inwardly when he felt himself actually blush. "Thanks. Feeling's mutual."

They finished their cigarettes and carried the crushed butts to the nearest metal trashcan. Then, whether he really wanted to or not, they finally joined the growing crowd in the front yard. Robbie groaned as dozens of kids ran around, hollerin' like whipped dogs, joined by the dogs themselves. The adults stood around in groups, chatting, drinking, nibbling on food. Across the yard littered with lawn chairs, card tables, and pear trees, Robbie spotted Danny and several others. Sure enough, Russ stood with them. God, his laughter felt like nails down a chalkboard.

"Robbie!" Kristy shouted, running to him and throwing skinny, pale arms around his neck.

Over her shoulder, Robbie met his brother's leering gaze. Kristy, Robbie could handle. Russ was another story entirely.

"How ya been, hun?"

"Tired from the drive," Robbie said, tearing away from Russ' stare to look down at Kristy. "Is it true?"

She sighed. "Yeah."

"You don't seem very happy about it," Robbie remarked.

Kristy looked up at him with an almost pleading look. That's when he saw the faintest outline of a bruise beneath her left eye. The entire world went blood-red.

Moving Kristy out of his way as carefully as possible, Robbie had one person and one person only in his sights. Before Russ knew what had happened, he was sprawled on the ground, probing a bloodied bottom lip.

"What the fuck was that for?" he shouted, blue eyes going near black.

Grabbing his shirt collar, Robbie hauled the bastard to his feet and slammed him against a tree, toppling several chairs and one small table with about five cups on it. Russ brought a knee up, but Robbie shifted. Instead of connecting with his balls, the impact hit his thigh. Still, it fucking hurt like hell. Movement out of the corner of his eye was his biggest mistake, though.

The second his attention was diverted, Russ managed to catch him in the jaw. Pain shot through Robbie's head and neck, but he shook it off, swallowing the bit of blood in his mouth.

"Robert! Russell!"

Robbie didn't have to look to know Mama was crying, but this was serious. He caught Russ' hand just before it could connect with his face. "You fucking hit her!"

"It's none of your fucking business, you goddamned faggot!" Russ screamed back.

Robbie's blood ran cold, and he threw his brother to the ground. Just as he raised his fist, with the sole intention of beating Russ to death, a strong arm wrapped around his waist, hauling him off of Russ. Danny had Russ, dragging him away as well. Russ screamed at the top of his lungs, names like 'faggot' and 'cock-sucking whore' and other things Robbie *really* didn't want anyone to hear, rolling off of the bastard's tongue like water.

"Hey!"

Robbie was spun around and met Seth's highly confused but very stern gaze. Then he saw Mama. The tears were clear as the morning sun. Before he could pull away to go to her, she was turning around and going back inside. Robbie looked around then, meeting several familiar—and concerned—faces. God. This was *not* happening. Not now.

Seth gripped his chin gently—on the good side—and turned Robbie's head. "He gotcha good, but I think you came out with the better end of the deal." He still had a firm hold on Robbie's arm.

"Will you please let go of me now?" Robbie grumbled.

"Will you go in the house and leave your bastard-of-a-brother be?"

Robbie nodded, and Seth let go of him. Taking one more look in his brother's direction, Robbie started towards the house. Seth followed close behind, although Robbie had a hunch it had nothing to do with lust. Smart man.

Chapter Four

"Mama?"

Robbie ignored the few others in the house as he looked for Mama. He continued to call for her as he started up the steps. When he reached the second-floor hallway, he heard soft sobs coming from one of the bedrooms down the hall.

"Mama?"

He found her there, back to the door and hunched over as she sat on the bed. Her shoulders were trembling, and she sniffled several times. As Robbie walked around the bed, he saw a photo album open in her lap. Pictures of his family—of her, him, Russ, and Dad—covered the pages, edge to edge. Lord, this was not going to be easy.

He sat down beside her, pushing a bit of gray hair away and tucking it behind her left ear. "Mama, I'm so sorry."

"Oh, Robbie!" Mama turned into his arms and he held her, kissing her hair softly. "Why?"

Robbie didn't ask. He had a good feeling the 'why' applied to everything. He figured he'd start with the easy part.

"Kristy is bruised, Mama. Russ has been hitting her." Robbie swallowed hard as Mama wailed. The sound was choked and pitiful, but there was little he could really do. "It's not right, Mama."

"I know," she cried. "I know! I just can't believe my Russ would do that."

Robbie nodded. No matter how bad Russ was, he couldn't quite believe it himself. "Mama..." He sighed and closed his eyes. "Kristy's pregnant, too."

"I know that." Mama sighed. She raised her head and looked up at him. "She told me when they got here. She didn't want Russ to know that she told me either. Suppose I know why now."

Robbie managed a slight smile. "You always were easy to talk to, Mama," he said quietly, smoothing his hand over her hair.

"Was I?" The question, as innocent as it was, stung deep. "Why didn't you tell me?"

"Because some things are hard to talk about, to tell someone, no matter how much we love them," Robbie said. "Yes, Mama, I'm gay, but I'm happy and safe. I don't have any diseases, and I'm always careful. This is just a part of who I really am."

Mama sat quiet for so long that Robbie wondered if he was going to be told he was going to hell and to get out. Then Mama lifted a hand to his cheek and smiled.

"I love you, Robert," she said through her tears. "I don't understand it, but I accept it because you're my son."

Robbie let out a slow sigh of relief. "Thank you, Mama. I love you, too."

* * *

Eyes closed and heart heavy, Robbie pressed his forehead against the tiled wall of the shower. Steam and water helped to ease the slight aches of his body from the fight with Russ, but they didn't begin to touch what hurt on the inside. He had planned on coming out to Mama soon, but not like that. And definitely not the day before his dad's funeral.

"How'd it go?" A soft kiss brushed to the top of his shoulder, and his hair was pulled to the side. Seth's lips followed the curve of his neck.

Robbie sighed, then moaned softly as Seth bit down on his neck just enough to send a tingle of sweet pain through him. "As well as can be expected, I guess. She doesn't understand why I'm gay, but she loves me and accepts me." Robbie reached back, gripping Seth's hip to pull him closer.

"That's a good start." Seth's lips drifted across Robbie's skin in a soft caress. It was a sharp contrast to the long, thick hardness pressing against Robbie's backside. "Anything I can do?"

Now there was a loaded question if he ever heard one. Robbie laughed as the afternoon's excursion into hell was soon replaced with an almost aching need for a tall, tanned cowboy. He spread his legs slightly, and, acting on the clear invitation, Seth slid up against him, cock slipping between Robbie's legs. Robbie gasped, body tightening as several inches of rock hard silk slid under his balls, his cock.

He tilted his head back and to the side, meeting Seth in a slow, deep kiss. A moan slipped from one of them, but Robbie could no longer tell which one of them had made it. It seemed they were one body, all parts moving together, breaths shared between them. The kiss left Robbie dizzy and wanting as Seth pulled away slowly.

"Want you so bad," Seth whispered against his shoulder. Kisses moved along Robbie's back, Seth's tongue tracing the path as he went. "Back up a little."

With Seth guiding him, hands on his hips, Robbie backed up and leaned forward, resting his forehead against the shower wall again. Seth knelt down behind him, and Robbie felt the cowboy's lips on his right buttock. A moan escaped him as Seth spread him open, letting the water slide down the crease of his ass. Then that sweet tongue was inside him, lapping the water from his hole like it was the nectar of the gods. Robbie gasped and whimpered, rocking back as Seth's tongue pushed inside again.

"Seth. Oh, God."

Robbie's legs were growing weak, and he had a hell of a time trying to keep himself upright. His heart thundered as Seth's tongue worked him, plunging deep inside, sucking gently on the tender, puckered skin. Then the warmth of Seth's mouth was gone. Robbie groaned in frustration until a finger touched him, pressing just enough to tease.

"Wanna be inside you, Robbie." Seth's gasp echoed Robbie's as he pushed his finger inside. Curling his finger forward, Seth chuckled as a hard shudder slid straight up Robbie's spine.

Robbie dropped a hand down to touch himself, but Seth swatted his hand away. "Oh, God. Please."

Without removing his finger, Seth stood slowly, kissing his way back up Robbie's body. "Want something else in there?" He stroked Robbie's gland lightly, and Robbie cried out, body jerking.

"Yes! Please, yes!" Robbie reached down with a shaking hand and turned off the water. "Towel," he panted, unable to think too clearly when Seth seemed intent on driving him to the point of begging.

"No towel," Seth said. He curled his other arm around Robbie's waist and stepped out of the tub, pulling Robbie with him, finger still buried in Robbie's ass. "Walk."

"Yeah." Robbie laughed, head reeling. Every step he took was torture, and Seth wasn't helping in the least. Every two steps, he'd give Robbie's gland another stroke, nearly sending Robbie to his knees. By the time they reached the bed, Robbie was sweating, breath far from steady, body aching.

"On your back."

Finally getting away from Seth's finger, Robbie stretched out on the bed. He watched as Seth fumbled around in his jeans. When Seth pulled out several condom packages, Robbie couldn't help but laugh.

"Ulterior motives?"

Seth crawled onto the bed, parting Robbie's legs slowly. "You could say that."

Robbie didn't get a chance to say anything else. Seth's tongue pushed into his mouth, swallowing his moans as their cocks moved together, the clear drops slicking them both. Robbie reached down and kneaded Seth's ass, a buttock in each hand, spreading and squeezing them. Seth groaned and shifted until his cock slipped down to press against Robbie's hole.

"Lube. Box on the table," Robbie gasped.

Seth sat up on his knees and found the lube. Then he was sheathed and slick, mouth crashing onto Robbie's in a hungrier kiss than before. Robbie moaned and spread his legs more, rocking his hips up. Head pressing against his hole, Seth's cock pierced his body in one slow push.

"Oh, my God." Robbie's back bowed, his legs going up to lock around Seth's waist, tugging him deeper. "Seth. Oh, fuck..."

"Yes." Seth met him in another kiss, tongue fucking his mouth with deep, slow strokes.

Giving the corner of Robbie's mouth another kiss, Seth rose up onto his hands. Gazes locked, blue to green, they began to move, slow and easy. Robbie stroked his hands up and down Seth's arms, lingering over the hard biceps, the broad shoulders. Every time Seth's long cock filled him, it took Robbie's breath away, stretching him so much that he thought he would die from the pleasure alone.

Hand moving to stroke his cock, Robbie jerked himself off, matching Seth's movements stroke for stroke. When Seth's thrusts became harder and quicker, Robbie's body tightened, his balls drawing up to his body as he neared released. His breath was erratic and heavy, and sweat beaded on his chest, on Seth's. Then Seth leaned down and caught the silver ring in Robbie's left nipple between his teeth.

"Fuck!" Robbie jerked and arched up as he came, heat shooting over his chest, splashing on Seth's.

Seth growled. Several hard, quick thrusts drove him deep inside Robbie's ass, and he came. Robbie gasped, and his eyes widened as Seth's cock nailed his prostate. He dragged his fingernails down Seth's back, body shaking, voice hoarse as he cried out Seth's name. Seth kissed him hard, grunts and growls filling Robbie's mouth as the pulsing of his cock began to slow.

As they both slowly came back to Earth, Robbie slid his legs down, still cradling Seth between them while they kissed. The kisses were slow and easy, and they stroked each other, fingers twisting and sliding through hair and over work-hardened muscles.

"Damn." Robbie shook his head. "Just...damn."

Seth laughed and slipped out of him, pulled off the rubber, then rolled onto one side. Draping a long, muscular arm around Robbie, Seth pulled him close. Robbie turned and curled around the cowboy's body, a soft sound of contentment escaping him. He had almost dozed off when Seth's voice pulled him out of it.

"So what are you going to do here? Get a job in town?"

"Mack needs some help, and I need immediate work. Might not be art-related, but a job's a job." He looked up at Seth. "Why?"

Seth shrugged. "Was kina hopin' you'd stick around here, 'round the farm." Brilliant green eyes met Robbie's, and something within them made his heart jump just a bit.

"Why?"

Seth caught his hand just as it started making absent swirls over the cowboy's chest. "Maybe because I'm partial to you?"

"Yeah?" Robbie smiled. "Likewise."

Grabbing his shoulders, Seth flipped him over onto his back with a growl. Robbie's laughter morphed into soft moans as Seth slid down his body, lips and tongue caressing his chest, his stomach. Skipping his awakening cock entirely, Seth dropped light kisses to Robbie's thighs, mouth drifting higher again until Seth could trace the inner crease of Robbie's hip with his tongue.

Work-rough hands cupped his balls, and Robbie gasped, legs spreading. He slid his fingers through the cowboy's brown hair, nudging Seth with his hips, desperate for a touch. When

Seth sucked one of Robbie's balls into his mouth and tugged, Robbie's entire body arched.

"Nice tats," Seth chuckled when he released Robbie. "I take it you designed these, too." He traced the outline of the triskele between Robbie's navel and cock. "What does this one mean?"

It took a minute for Robbie's brain to catch up and process an answer. "It's a triskele," he said, picturing the triple, interlocking spirals. "It's a Celtic symbol representing Earth, Sea, and Sky, among other spiritual trinities."

"Interesting." Seth slid up a bit, and Robbie groaned as Seth traced the outline of the spirals with his tongue. "And this one?" Seth brushed his fingertips down the length of Robbie's cock, over his balls, and finally to his right thigh where an ivy vine curled around his leg.

"That one was just because I liked it," Robbie whispered breathlessly. "Oh, God." His hips rose off of the bed as Seth swallowed him down without warning, nose rubbing in the light brown hair around the base of his cock. "Don't stop. Oh, God, don't stop."

Lips tightening around his shaft, Seth slid slowly back up to the head, teeth scraping slightly. Robbie hissed and jerked as the head was given a tight, sucking kiss. Then before he could blink, Seth had a condom unrolled onto his prick and was slicking it up, fist sliding up and down the shaft.

"All cowboys like to ride," Seth said with a wink. Moving back up, he straddled Robbie, then sank down.

"Oh, fuck..." Robbie gripped Seth's hips as the velvet heat sucked him in. Cock buried balls-deep inside Seth, Robbie groaned. "Dear Lord, you're tight."

"Been a while." Seth leaned down, tongue dipping into Robbie's mouth, tasting, exploring. "Fuck me," he whispered.

Without wasting another second on talking, Robbie pulled his legs up, anchoring his feet firmly on the bed. Hands on Seth's hips, he guided their movements as Seth rode his cock. With every thrust inside, Robbie pulled Seth down. He rocked his hips up, pegging Seth's gland every time.

"God, Robbie, don't stop," Seth panted. He started pumping his cock hard and fast, chest rising and falling. "Yes!"

Robbie jerked and shouted, cock throbbing as Seth's body squeezed every last drop from him. Seth collapsed onto his chest, heedless of the sticky mess between them. Robbie closed his eyes, mind completely scrambled beyond reason. He'd needed this, needed every damn second of it.

Chapter Five

The funeral had been rough, to say the least. The church had been filled to capacity with friends and family—people whose lives Gerald Sexton touched. Robbie had sat with Mama and made damn sure Kristy sat with them. Russ stayed in the back, conveniently out of sight for the most part. And on Robbie's left sat a cowboy, black hat in his lap out of respect. Something about having Seth with him, even when the majority of the tears came from Mama, was a comfort. Robbie never cried in front of anyone. When he and Seth got out of the church, though, inside Seth's truck, Robbie broke down. They sat there in the church parking lot, Robbie soaking the front of Seth's white dress shirt, his dark blue tie. No one batted an eye at them.

Back at the farm, Mama was made to take it easy while others waited on her, Robbie reluctant to leave her side. As well-wishers came and went, offering condolences, Mama seemed to be smiling a bit more. Robbie was grateful for that, for family and friends. Across the yard, he met the green gaze of a cowboy. Black Stetson tipped back just enough to see his face, Seth leaned against a tree, arms crossed as he watched and smiled.

"Oh, for Heaven's sake. Go to him already."

Robbie blinked and looked down at Mama. "What?"

Mama sat back in the rocking chair and laughed until her face was pink. "You think I haven't noticed?"

Looking from her to Seth, then back to her, Robbie was simply stunned. They had been so careful. "Noticed...?"

"Noticed how you two look at each other," Mama said with a knowing smile that only a mother could give. "He even sat with you during your daddy's funeral." She leaned forward. "He held you when you cried. Now that, son, is a good man."

Robbie's mouth dropped open. "We were so careful..."

"Ah," Mama said, lifting a finger, "but I am your Mama, Robert Sexton. Man or woman, I know when someone is smitten over my son."

"We just met..." Robbie's words trailed off as he looked back at Seth. The man hadn't moved, but that look was back in Seth's eyes, that look...of something much more. "It never really crossed my mind."

"Nonsense," Mama said. She swatted Robbie's rear. "Get over there. You know just as well as I do that he's everything you want. And there he is, offering it all to you."

Robbie leaned down and kissed Mama on the head, then walked down the porch steps. As he crossed the yard towards Seth, he thought about what Mama had said. Did he really dare think that something more could come of this? When he stopped a few feet from Seth, he thought he just might dare to try.

"Come on," Seth said. "There's a spot I'd like to show *you* where a man can find peace."

Robbie laughed and followed him, not bothering to hide the fact that he was staring at the cowboy's firm ass in tight Wranglers. Seth still wore his white dress shirt, but his tie hung loose around his neck. His dark brown boots, which had been polished for the funeral, reflected the sun as they walked across the yard. Tearing his gaze away from Seth's body, Robbie looked around. Seth led the way towards one of the hay barns. Robbie grinned.

Both of them took a quick glance around before slipping through the door of the barn. Hay squares were stacked from floor to ceiling, some stacks threatening to topple over. Robbie breathed deep, sighing as the thick, rich scent filled him. It brought back memories of building hay forts and sneaking kisses in dark corners. When he looked back at Seth, he found the man sitting on a large bed of golden brown straw—eight bales set together in a rectangle, just wide enough and long enough for two grown men. Robbie cocked an eyebrow as he started over to Seth.

"Hey, ya don't think I've been sitting on my ass, do you?" Seth teased. Reaching out, fingers lacing with Robbie's, Seth tugged him down.

Robbie landed on his back and moaned as Seth straddled him, cocks rubbing together through too much clothing. Seth's kiss was soft but deep, easy as his tongue caressed Robbie's mouth, tasting and touching. There was no hurry in it, no driving urge to get off; only the slow-simmering desire between them. Pulling away slowly, Seth stared down at him, green eyes going dark.

"What?" Robbie asked him, tilting his head just a bit so that Seth's head blocked the flash of sunlight shining through a hole in the barn's tin roof. Golden light surrounded Seth's head like one of those halos in the pictures of saints Robbie had seen throughout childhood. The effect seemed oddly fitting.

Brow furrowing, Seth looked quite pensive. "Is there any chance of something more coming of this?"

For several minutes, all Robbie could do was stare into those deep emerald eyes. *Was* there a chance? He certainly hoped so. He nodded slowly. "Was kinda hopin' so."

Seth smiled and leaned down for another kiss. This one started out like the first—slow and easy, more exploring than hunger. Then Seth moved against him, and Robbie gasped, cock filling and libido going from a low simmer to a rolling boil within seconds. The kiss turned hungry then, Seth groaning into his mouth, hips rocking as Robbie's hands settled on them, pushing and pulling. Seth broke the kiss and descended on Robbie's neck, growling and grunting, biting and licking the sensitive skin just where Robbie's neck met his shoulder.

"Fuck," Robbie hissed.

Seth slid a hand between them and began unbuttoning Robbie's dress shirt. Robbie tugged Seth's shirt out of his jeans, wanting—*needing*—to feel skin. Once his shirt was open, Robbie groaned as Seth's mouth drifted over his collarbone, tongue licking his skin. Then that tongue flicked his nipple ring. Robbie grunted and arched his body, thrusting his chest up. Seth caught the ring in his teeth and tugged, sending bolts of lightning from Robbie's nipple to his cock.

Fingers tightening in Seth's hair, Robbie rock his body under the cowboy's, moaning and gasping as Seth sucked on his nipple, tugging and nibbling the ring. Robbie's cock jumped with every pull.

"Back pocket," Seth muttered against Robbie's chest.

Robbie blinked several times, his brain beyond scrambled. "Huh?"

Seth lifted his head and looked down at him, the movements of his hips slowing but not stopping completely.

It was just enough to keep Robbie riding the slow wave of building pleasure without coming too close to the breaking point.

"Stuff in my back pocket," Seth said. "Always prepared."

Robbie grinned, and a slow shudder stole up his spine. He ran both hands down Seth's ass, watching the way those eyes darkened a bit with need. When he felt the small square outline, he slipped his hand into the pocket to get it out.

"Want you inside me," Seth whispered, lips brushing his.

Robbie could only nod. Seth stood, shoving jeans and underwear down, kicking his boots off. Robbie quickly followed suit and stood up to spread their shirts and jeans out to give Seth a little more cushion from the prickly hay. He set the rubber aside. As Seth lay back, Robbie dropped to his knees. First things first: he wanted to taste.

"Robbie..."

Seth's fingers curled in Robbie's hair as Robbie tongued Seth's balls, sucking first one and then the other into his mouth. Sweet and salty and all man. He could die just like this—Seth in his mouth—and he'd be perfectly content. He let Seth slip free and licked lower, pressing his tongue just behind Seth's balls to the small bit of flesh between them and his ass. Seth jerked and groaned, pulling his legs up and apart. Robbie leaned back just enough to watch the cowboy spread himself open, pink hole utterly mouth-watering. Without another thought, Robbie dove in, licking the puckered rim before pushing inside with his tongue, moaning against Seth's flesh as the musky male scent bombarded his senses.

"Robbie, don't stop..."

Robbie spent longer fucking Seth with his tongue than he ever had with anyone else. Seth's taste was strong, mouth-watering, and unbelievably addictive. Oh, yeah. He could live with this for a long time. But his cock had other ideas. It bobbed between his legs, tip leaking, drops coating the hay-strewn floor. He gave Seth's ass one more flick of his tongue, then stood. Seth scooted back just enough for Robbie to kneel on the hay between his legs. Robbie got his cock covered, grinning when Seth handed him a tiny little bottle. Robbie chuckled. Always prepared indeed. After squirting a bit of lube into his hand, Robbie stroked himself, caught in an intense, hungry stare with a sun god. *His* sun god, all spread out for him, body flushed, cock hard and leaking, ass glistening with spit and ready for him.

Leaning forward, Robbie pushed his tongue into Seth's mouth just as he pushed his cock into the cowboy's body. Seth groaned and bore down, muscles straining and stretching, drawing him in deeper.

"Robbie."

Name whispered against his own lips, Robbie shuddered. He slid his hands down until he found Seth's, then he pulled them both up above Seth's head, linking their fingers together. A soft sound—possibly a whimper—passed between them. Robbie began moving, rocking his hips slowly, cock hard and balls heavy as he pierced Seth's body with deep, gentle strokes. The tight heat closing around him, caressing his shaft, spurred Robbie on.

"Yes," Seth whispered breathlessly as Robbie sped up.

Seth's fingers tightened around his as every thrust drove Robbie deeper into that blazing heat. Releasing one of Seth's hands, Robbie reached between them, hips never stopping their quickening movements as he began stroking Seth's cock. Seth's eyes went wide, and he jerked hard, shouting Robbie's name as his cock spilled over Robbie's fist. As Seth's muscles worked his cock, gripping and pulling, Robbie lost all control. One more thrust, and he crushed his mouth to Seth's as he came, Seth's body milking him for all he was worth.

Finally, Robbie broke the kiss and dropped his head to Seth's chest. Easing out of Seth, he let out a ragged sigh and slipped off the rubber. He tied it closed and dropped it on the floor. Then he relaxed back on top of Seth as the man stroked his back, his sides, fingers sliding slowly upwards to comb through his hair, tugging the ponytail free. Robbie moaned softly as Seth massaged his scalp, then his neck, his shoulders.

"That...was unbelievable," Robbie whispered against Seth's chest. He felt Seth nod and kiss his hair.

"Yeah. It was."

This was well worth coming home for.

Part Two: August, 2006
Chapter Six

Dawn came entirely too fucking early. Robbie had never been a morning person.

"What possessed me to do this?"

Seth chuckled, and Robbie stared up at him.

"Fuck if I know." Seth ruffled his fingers through Robbie's hair. "Come on. Rise and shine."

"It's too damn early," Robbie grumbled as he tossed back the covers.

"You'll get used to it." Seth gave him a grin and a once-over that set Robbie's pulse racing.

"Keep staring at me like that, Cowboy, and you'll be back in bed."

Seth bent, bringing their mouths together for a good-morning kiss. Robbie hummed his appreciation, slid an arm around Seth's neck, and tugged. Seth made a surprised noise as he landed on his back on the bed. Robbie grinned down at him and licked his cowboy's lips, receiving a guttural groan for his attention.

"Warned you," Robbie murmured, moving down that muscled body. He pushed Seth's shirt up, moaning when his hands and lips met warm, tanned skin. "So hot..."

"Robbie."

Robbie grumbled. "Do we really have to get up?"

Seth tugged him back up and planted a kiss on his lips. "Yes."

"Damn it." Robbie sighed and kissed Seth one more time before getting out of bed. "I need a shower. Wanna join me?"

"If I do, we'll never make it out," Seth said. "I'll meet you downstairs."

Robbie stuck his tongue out and wandered into the bathroom.

* * *

Seth shook his head and laughed before heading down to the kitchen. "Hey, boys!"

"Damn, looks like someone got lucky last night." Jack, one of the other ranch hands, sat down with a mug of coffee. "Lemme guess, Mack's nephew?"

"You know it." Seth got out two mugs and fixed two cups of coffee. "He's not used to this early morning stuff, though."

Ty, the other live-in ranch hand, snorted as he walked into the kitchen. "Guess we'll just have to change that, won't we?"

"He learns quick," Seth said. "He'll pick it up."

Jack snickered. "Especially with *you* showing him."

Ty looked from one man to another. "Did I miss something?"

"Might as well know now," Jack said. "Seth staked his claim on Mack's nephew."

Ty's eyes went wide, and he stared at Seth. "I didn't know you were gay."

"He's queer as a football bat." Jack set his coffee mug in the sink.

Seth rolled his eyes and looked back at Ty. "I just keep it quiet, ya know? Not many take it well."

"I can get that," Ty said, nodding.

"Get what?" Robbie padded into the kitchen in jeans and a dark blue T-shirt, his wet hair pulled back into a ponytail.

"Well, well, speak of the devil." Jack's grin was wide and teasing. He got up and slapped Seth's shoulder. "You gonna...show 'im the *ropes*, Seth?"

Glaring at Jack, Seth just shook his head. "Get out of here. We'll see y'all at lunchtime."

"Yeah, yeah." Ty grinned and left the kitchen with Jack.

"Do I want to know?"

"They find it utterly amusing we're together." Seth handed Robbie his coffee and took a drink of his own. He held out a hand and rumbled happily when Robbie stepped up to him, pushing close for a kiss. "Mm, morning again."

"Morning. I take it we're okay around them?"

"Yes, at least with those two. Hell, Jack's family," Seth said before finishing off his coffee. "But some of the others who don't live on-site may not be too friendly toward us. Just be careful, and you should be okay."

"Cool. So what's on the schedule first?"

"Need to check the work board." Seth set his mug in the sink and slipped both arms around Robbie's waist. "But first..."

Robbie didn't give him a chance to finish, just pressed right up to him and kissed him senseless. Seth hummed into the kiss, tongue sweeping through Robbie's mouth. He didn't think he'd ever get tired of kissing this man.

"I wish we had more time," Robbie murmured, pushing a hand between them and cupping Seth's hardening prick through his jeans.

Seth groaned when Robbie squeezed his shaft. "Fuck. I can't think when you do that."

Robbie chuckled and licked Seth's lips, nipping at the bottom one. "Not supposed to be thinking."

Seth had to stop them both before they got going. He grabbed Robbie's hand and lifted it to his mouth, kissing Robbie's fingers. "I'd say 'hell, yes' any other time, but we got work to do."

Groaning in disappointment, Robbie nodded. "Yeah, I know. Sucks."

Seth chuckled. He gave Robbie another kiss and let him go. "C'mon. Let's see what needs to be done."

* * *

If there was one thing Robbie figured out fast, it was that the day went by quickly when doing manual labor. By lunchtime, he'd learned how to replace a fence section, where *not* to walk in a pasture, and how to build the world's ultimate hay fort.

Okay, so the hay fort wasn't exactly work. It was, however, ungodly amusing to see three grown men argue over the strategic placement of a block of straw. Robbie leaned back on the grass, grinning like mad at the scene playing out in front of him.

"I'm tellin' you, it needs to be wide 'n long."

Jack shook his head at Ty. "You're nuts, boy. Tall, so you can't be shot."

"I think you're both screwed," Seth said, legs dangling off from where he sat up on the monstrous tire of a tractor, just outside the barn door. He took a slow drag from his Marlboro and winked at Robbie as he blew out the smoke. "Tall, long, and thick...that's what you want."

Robbie barely swallowed his groan. The image those words conjured up had his jeans tightening unbearably. Seth just flashed him a knowing grin.

Jake and Ty both looked up at Seth.

"All right, cowboy," Jack challenged. "Get your ass down here and demonstrate your fine architectural skills."

"Gladly." Seth jumped from the top of the tire, booted feet kicking up dust when he landed. He waved both men away, mumbling, "Move on, move on." He handed Robbie his cigarette.

"You realize a hay fort is the last thing on my mind now," Robbie muttered under his breath. Looking up, he stared into too-green eyes.

"Gives you somethin' to look forward to come quittin' time, baby." Seth's grin was wicked as he turned around, heading to the fort.

Robbie watched that sweet-as-fuck, denim-encased ass saunter away, and he had to cross his legs to hide the terminal hard-on. Since meeting a month ago, they couldn't keep their hands off of each other, it seemed. Then again, at least to Robbie, it felt as if he'd known Seth all his life.

"Watch the *Master*," Seth announced. Grunting, he lifted another bale and set it down on top of one of the others.

Fifteen minutes and countless bales later, a huge fort dominated the ground floor of the barn. In height, it was one bale taller than Seth—well over six feet—and it completely circled Ty and Jack, both of whom stood slack-jawed and staring. The walls were two bales wide and gave them both plenty of room to move around in.

"Well, I'll be damned," Ty said, scratching his head. "Guess he was right: tall, long, and thick."

Jack smacked the back of Ty's head. "Well, duh."

"Hey!" Ty glared at Jack. "You weren't right either, asshole."

"More than you."

"Oh, for fuck's sake." Seth rolled his eyes and stepped out of the barn to light up. The cigarette bobbed up and down, caught between those sinfully tempting lips as Seth talked. "You both were wrong."

"Time to get back to work," Robbie said as he stood.

"Yep." Seth's gaze never left his as Robbie met his cowboy halfway. "Got a new tractor Mack wants me to go look at. Wanna come?"

"Oh. Do I ever," Robbie murmured. God, he wanted a kiss, but work first. "Let's go."

"See ya boys later!" Seth waved, winking at Robbie when Jack and Ty both started yellin' about a way out of the fort.

Robbie followed him over to the truck and climbed in, buckling as Seth slid in the driver's side. "Will they ever stop arguing long enough to just take the damn thing apart?"

Seth held the cigarette in his lips as he started the truck. As he buckled, he just shook his head. He put the truck into gear, released the emergency brake, and started down the road leading to the highway. "Not a fucking chance," he said finally, grinning around the cigarette. "If Jack had his way, they'd never leave."

"Seriously?"

Seth nodded. "He's had it bad for Ty for, well, at least since I've been here."

"Huh. Learn something new every day," Robbie said. "So what was that about 'tall, long, and thick?'" He reached over and slid one hand along Seth's right thigh. He got a heated look from the corner of Seth's eye.

"That an offer?" Seth didn't wait for an answer, just reached down and popped the button on his jeans.

Oh, fuck yes.

Robbie said a quick prayer for no cops, unbuckled, and shifted until he could semi-comfortably get his head where it needed to be. He hadn't done anything this risky since high school. He eased Seth's zipper down and inhaled deeply, savoring the scent of sweat and need pouring off his cowboy. When he pulled out Seth's cock, he gave it a long, lingering look, loving the way the flared head oozed those sweet, clear drops when he squeezed.

"Robbie..." Seth's voice was deep and rumbling, full of need and a touch of warning for Robbie to hurry the hell up.

Robbie happily obliged.

Opening his mouth, he licked away the drops, and then dropped down the shaft, lips circling, throat working to swallow as much of Seth as he could. He got a low groan for his efforts, one of Seth's hands combing through his hair, urging his head up and down. Breathing through his nose, Robbie gave his sun god what the man wanted. Up and down, in and out, he worked Seth good, tongue caressing the sensitive underside, teeth grazing just slightly, Seth's hips pushing up just a bit.

"Fuck..."

Robbie felt the truck veer off the road and stop. Then both of Seth's hands were in his hair, his cowboy panting, moaning, pushing that sweet, thick cock deeper into his mouth. Robbie groaned and humped the truck's bench seat. Seth's fingers tightened in his hair, the rhythm turning quick and sharp. Then Seth was coming, slick heat pouring down Robbie's throat, Seth almost chanting his name.

Robbie moaned and barely managed to stop before making a total mess of his jeans. He licked Seth clean and pulled off the thick cock, dropping his head to his cowboy's thigh.

"Damn." Seth groaned. "So fucking good, baby. So fucking good."

Robbie nodded, loving Seth's hands on his head, petting him. So fucking good.

* * *

Robbie stayed off to the side, pretending to browse and trying like hell not to look bored out of his skull. He was so far out of his element, he felt like a newly-landed alien. Seth was still talking with the salesman, both men working each other over on pricing. If anything, Robbie figured his cowboy knew his shit. When he finally reached the point of running out of stuff to browse, Robbie settled back against an enormous tire and just admired the view.

Seth was a god. There was absolutely no doubt in Robbie's mind of that. The man could turn anything into gold with only a smile. Robbie felt the knot forming in his stomach before it really hit him: he was head-over-heels in love with Seth Ellis.

He'd been in lust many times, but never had he felt like this. Certainly not so soon. Did love at first sight really exist?

The men finally shook hands a few minutes later, and Seth sauntered back over to Robbie, grinning.

"That looked like it went well."

Seth nodded and pulled a cell phone from his jeans pocket. Flipping it open, he hit a couple of buttons. "Hey, Mack. Talked him down." He paused and waved Robbie toward the parking lot. "Yeah, here he is." Seth handed the phone to Robbie while tugging his keys from his other pocket.

Robbie took the phone. "Hey."

"Robbie, your mama called."

Robbie felt that knot grow into something bigger, turning bad. "Everything okay?"

"Afraid not, son," Mack said. "Kristy's in the hospital."

"What happened?" Robbie got into the truck, and Seth closed the door for him.

Mack sighed. "Russ is on the run, Robbie. He beat her, bad."

The phone slipped out of Robbie's hand and landed on the floor between his feet. Seth picked it up and started the truck. Robbie barely heard Seth's voice as they pulled out of the parking lot, his cowboy doing more listening than talking.

"I'll get him there, Mack. You sure you don't need me?" Seth pulled out onto the highway and headed in the opposite direction of home. "We'll call. Bye." He snapped the phone shut and just reached over, fingers gripping Robbie's tightly, reassuring.

Robbie was just...numb.

The drive to Athens-Limestone Hospital was quiet, Seth's hand never leaving Robbie's. Once they were parked and the truck was off, Robbie just stared, not quite remembering the ride at all.

"Hey," Seth said softly. "We're here, baby."

"I'll kill him."

Seth's other hand cupped Robbie's chin, turning it until Robbie found himself staring into green eyes full of concern and sympathy. "I know. I would, too."

No talking him out of it, no lectures on getting arrested, just his cowboy nodding, understanding the rage. The words left Robbie's lips before he even realized it.

"I love you."

Seth smiled and leaned in for a slow, soft kiss. "Good, 'cause I'm here to stay, Robbie. Love you, too."

A small, almost desperate sound escaped Robbie, and the pain, the rage, everything faded with Seth's kiss. When they came up for air, Seth gave him a little smile.

"C'mon, babe. Your mama and Kristy need you."

Nodding, Robbie got out and waited for Seth. They went in together, his cowboy's hand tight on his. Robbie walked up to the information desk, but before he could even open his mouth, he saw Mama. Her face was streaked with tears, and she looked like she'd aged about ten years. Seth let go of him, and Robbie went to her, pulling her close and holding her. Robbie just let her cry. When she pulled back, she smiled weakly up at him.

"Hi, baby. She's..."

"Shh, I'm here, Mama."

She took a long, ragged breath and smiled over at Seth. "Hi, Seth, darlin'."

Seth nodded and slipped off his hat. "Afternoon, ma'am."

"Can we see her?" Robbie asked.

Mama nodded. "Yeah. C'mon." When Seth tried to hang back, she grabbed his arm. "Oh, no, don't. You're a part of this family, too."

Seth's soft chuckle lightened the mood a little as Mama led them down a hall and to the elevators. "She's not in the ER?" he asked when she pushed the 'up' button.

"No. As soon as they knew the baby was good, they patched her up and put her in a regular room."

"How long has she been here?" Robbie couldn't believe it hadn't taken long.

Mama gave him a somewhat sheepish smile as they stepped into the elevator. "Since last night, baby. I wanted..." She took a deep breath before continuing. "I wanted to make sure she and the baby were okay first before I called."

They all fell silent, and a couple minutes later, the elevator dinged when they reached their floor. Robbie and Seth followed Mama down the hall, past the nurses' station, and into a semi-dark room with a single bed.

Robbie hated hospitals; hated the way they looked, the way they smelled. He hated the feeling of helplessness they instilled in him, and the feeling worsened when he got his first look at Kristy. Seth's hand tightened on his.

Kristy looked bad, though Robbie figured it was an improvement from what the poor woman must've looked like when they first brought her in. Her nose was bandaged, as was her jaw. In fact, the white bandage was wrapped around her head. Her left eye was black and blue, swollen shut; and she was hooked up to all sorts of machines.

Robbie kind of tugged Seth behind him as he approached the bed slowly. Kristy was asleep and seemed to be breathing well. She wasn't on a ventilator of any kind, so that was a good thing. There was a heart monitor beside her bed, cords trailing under the blankets. He figured it was the baby's heart monitor. He watched and listened to each beep—healthy and steady.

"She's doing better, baby," Mama whispered from where she stood on the other side of the bed. "She just needs rest."

"Where's she going when she gets out?"

"She's coming to stay with me. I need the company, and she'll need the help the farther along she gets."

Robbie nodded, squeezed Seth's hand. "Okay. You know how to find me—"

"Find *us*," Seth interrupted.

Mama smiled. "I do," she said, nodding. "Y'all go on home. Get some rest. I'm staying here tonight. This chair behind me opens to a little bed."

"You'll call if you need us?" Robbie asked, looking up at her.

"I will." Mama walked around the bed and kissed Robbie, then Seth. "Go on. We'll be okay."

Robbie sighed, took another long look at Kristy, and nodded. "Love you, Mama."

"Love you, too."

Chapter Seven

Robbie rested his forehead against the tile wall of the shower and let the steaming water cascade down over him, washing away the rage and pain. Seth's hands were all over him, soap slicking the way, those fingers easing the tension in his muscles. A kiss brushed his shoulder, Seth's arms sliding around him, holding him tight.

"Thank you," Robbie whispered.

"I'd do anything for you," Seth murmured, mouth moving over Robbie's neck. "You know that, don't you?"

Robbie nodded, closed his eyes. "I know." He reached down and rested one hand over Seth's, just touching.

"What do you need?"

"I don't know." Robbie sighed. "Just know I need you right now."

Seth turned him around, fingers moving up to slide through Robbie's hair. "Do you trust me?" he whispered against Robbie's lips.

"Implicitly."

"I want to show you what it can be like to let go completely, to feel me deep inside you, filling you."

Robbie stared into his cowboy's eyes, those emeralds that took his breath away every time he looked into them. He knew damn well, just from the tone of Seth's voice, the words themselves, what the man meant. "Yes," he breathed, taking a kiss.

Seth groaned and pushed him back against the wall, tongue surging deep, sweeping through Robbie's mouth and stealing his breath, the last of his nervousness. He needed this; it was all he could think about as Seth's hands moved down to grip his hips, tugging him close to that long, hard body.

"I'll get things ready," Seth said, pulling back just enough for Robbie to see his face. "Love you."

Robbie smiled, body somewhere between needing and boneless. "Love you, too."

Seth leaned in for another kiss, then got out of the shower, wrapping one of the big towels around his waist. Robbie could hear him rummaging in the cabinet under the sink, getting things ready. Tipping his head back, Robbie exhaled slowly, eyes closed as the water sprayed down on his face. The depth of meaning behind what they were going to do took precedence in the forefront of his mind. It was probably the most intimate thing two people could do together, or at least that's what he thought. Actually doing it put any porn of it to shame. He shivered, already imagining Seth's fingers inside him, opening him up for more.

"Robbie?"

Robbie shook his head and turned off the water. He stepped out of the tub and saw Seth holding a hot water bottle set-up, though it sure as hell wasn't for relieving aches and pains. The nozzle was small, but still looked obscene. Goosebumps started to come up over Robbie's skin, and he could feel himself blushing.

"Trust me?" Seth asked him again, hanging the hook of the hot water bottle on the towel rack over the toilet.

Robbie swallowed. "Yeah."

"On your knees, put your head and shoulders to the floor," Seth said. "You know I won't do anything to hurt you."

"I know." Robbie got down on the towel-covered floor, assuming the position as instructed. A minute later, he felt Seth kneel behind him, one hand on his left buttock. He took a deep breath and let it out slowly.

"Just my finger, baby."

Robbie's hips instinctively rocked back, pushing Seth's slick finger deeper. A soft moan escaped him, and he shuddered as Seth moved the finger in and out, fucking him with it. Then Seth's finger was gone, and slick, slender plastic took its place.

"Ready?"

He nodded, and there was a soft click. Water began filling him. Seth held the nozzle in place with one hand and stroked the other over Robbie's stomach, soothing. When the pressure grew stronger, Seth stopped the water flow and removed the nozzle.

"Just let it set for a few," Seth said, leaning down to kiss the small of Robbie's back. "I'll be in the bedroom, getting things together. Come out when you're ready."

"Okay," Robbie mumbled, groaning slightly when a tiny cramp set in.

After a few minutes, Robbie finished up. He got back in the shower long enough to give himself one more wash-over. When done, he went into the bedroom, towel around his hips.

Seth knelt on the bed. Another towel was spread out in front of him, and there was a bottle of lube on the bed beside him. But the one thing that set Robbie's heart racing was the latex glove on Seth's right hand. Something about the way Seth watched, the way the man waited, made Robbie think his cowboy had done this—and possibly more—many, many times.

Robbie couldn't help but shiver as he let the towel drop to the floor. Crawling onto the bed, he lay down on his back, legs spread. He was so hard it hurt, and his body tingled everywhere, the anticipation unbelievable.

"Wanna come now?" Seth asked him. "Take the edge off?"

Robbie shook his head, gaze riveted on Seth's hand as his cowboy slicked it up. The sound was erotic as hell, that crinkle of latex as Seth coated the gloved hand in lube. Then the bottle was set aside, and Seth scooted up, resting on his knees.

"I'll go as slow as you want me to."

Nodding, Robbie inhaled, then exhaled, but try as he might, he couldn't get the tremors to stop. His thighs trembled as Seth's finger circled his ass, pushed slowly inside.

"Look at me," Seth whispered, working a second finger in. "It's part of the experience, for both of us."

Robbie licked his lips and stared into Seth's eyes, hips rolling slightly as a third finger joined the first two. Three had always been his limit.

"You okay?"

He nodded and let his legs fall apart, going slack as possible.

"Adding the fourth finger."

Robbie never looked away, gaze locked onto Seth's as a fourth finger pushed in, stretching him open. He drew in a breath when Seth scissored them gently, spreading him, working his hole.

"Seth..."

"Shhh, I'm here, baby." Seth coaxed his body to open more, fingers moving, spreading, sliding.

Robbie began slipping off into another world, the sensations too much to keep his eyes open. Seth's fingertips grazed lightly over his prostate, but didn't linger, just touching enough to make Robbie gasp, make his hips rock a little. In and out, in and out, Seth took things slow, working his body. Robbie steadied his breathing, in and out in an easy, calm rhythm, the world far away from this time and place.

"Let me in."

Robbie heard Seth, though he seemed far away. A bit of pressure, a twist of Seth's wrist, and the world disappeared entirely. Robbie's mind shorted out as his body sucked Seth's hand into him. His mouth opened on a soundless scream, and awareness snapped back: Seth, him, Seth's hand inside him. It was too much, too intense...

Tears filled Robbie's eyes as he bucked, rocked, driving Seth's fist deeper, fucking himself on it until his entire existence exploded. He jerked and squeezed Seth's hand, sobbing out Seth's name as he came.

Shaking and incoherent, Robbie slumped down onto the bed. He felt Seth's hand ease out of him. Then strong arms were around him, holding him tightly as he just fell apart.

* * *

"How's she doin'?"

Seth glanced up to see Mack Sexton standing in the stall doorway. "Best as can be expected."

"Robbie?"

Looking out at the truck, Seth watched Robbie shimmy under it. Only God knew what the blazes Jack had Robbie doing.

"He's taking it hard," Seth said finally. "He cares a lot for Kristy, and he's lookin' forward to being an uncle, I think."

"Robbie always was a good kid."

Seth looked over at Mack. "Did you know about him before?"

Mack chuckled. "I wondered a few times. Robbie never showed any interest in the girls."

"You're a unique man," Seth said with a smile.

"Bah." Mack shrugged. "I'm too old to get bent out of shape, payin' attention to others' issues." He winked. "Besides, I might've been curious in college."

Seth's mouth just sort of dropped open, and Mack walked away, laughing. Mack? Bisexual? Seth couldn't quite get those words to form any sort of cohesive thought. No wonder the man hadn't batted an eye when Seth had been upfront about his sexuality at the start. Turning back to the stall and shaking his head, Seth nailed the last support for the new trough into place. A few minutes later, something cold seeped right through his shirt, chilling a line up his back.

"What the fuck?"

A crotch, hard and demanding, pressed against his ass and a beer bottle dangled in front of his face. Taking the bottle, Seth straightened back up. He glanced over his shoulder toward the truck where the others had been, saw no one, and reached back. Tipping his head to the side, he groaned when Robbie's lips fastened onto the curve of his neck.

"Where'd the others go?"

"Lunchtime," Robbie mumbled, licking a trail from Seth's neck to his ear. "They're inside."

Seth grinned and closed his eyes, fingers still clutching the neck of the bottle. "What did you have in mind?"

"Sucking you. Can't stop thinking about last night."

Robbie turned him around and pushed him back against the stall, tongue filling his mouth as fingers worked his jeans open. When Robbie took him in hand, Seth's legs weakened, and he panted into the kiss as Robbie slowly fisted his cock. Pulling away, Robbie just winked.

"Keep watch."

Then Robbie sank to his knees, sucking Seth down in one breath. Seth's eyes rolled back, but he fought to keep them open, intent on keeping watch even as he thrust into Robbie's mouth.

"Fuck, baby."

Robbie hummed, the vibration rippling around Seth's flesh like water.

Fuck, that mouth...

Seth moaned, fingers threading through Robbie's hair, catching when he reached the ponytail. He didn't pull it out, just held on, panting and groaning as Robbie worked his prick like the man had been born to do it. Lord, that mouth was sweet, perfect. Lips and tongue and the slightest hint of teeth; Seth knew he wouldn't last long.

The orgasm snuck up on him, and Seth's hips snapped forward, heat pouring down Robbie's throat. Robbie drank every drop and licked him clean.

"God, you taste fucking good."

Seth didn't have a chance to answer, just opened up for the kiss, groaning when he tasted the remnants of his come on Robbie's tongue. Hardness pressed against his thigh, Robbie almost humping his leg. Seth reached down and popped the button on Robbie's jeans, then pushed his hand inside, curling his fingers around that sweet prick.

"Seth..."

"Thinking about last night, huh?" Seth murmured, thumb pressing into the slit.

Robbie whimpered. Seth took another kiss and moved his other hand up under Robbie's shirt to tweak the ring in Robbie's nipple. Oh, the things he could do with that ring. He was rewarded with a jerk of his lover's hips and a moan. Another twist, and Robbie came, thrusting into Seth's hand.

"Damn." Robbie panted, breaking the kiss to let his head drop to Seth's shoulder.

Seth chuckled. "I agree." He brought his hand up to wipe it on the towel hanging over the stall, but Robbie caught it and began licking and sucking it clean. Seth stared at him, cock threatening to grow hard again.

"What you did last night," Robbie muttered, tongue washing away every last drop of come. "How many times have you done that before?"

Seth wasn't sure how to answer. "Long story."

Something flashed in Robbie's eyes. Curiosity? Longing maybe?

"Robbie? Seth?"

"Shit." Robbie scrambled to get himself tucked back in while Seth did the same.

"We're in here," Seth called out once they were both somewhat presentable.

Jack rounded the corner and stopped short. "I don't wanna know."

Robbie snorted. "No, probably not."

"What's up?" Seth asked.

"Uh, yeah..." Jack shook his head. "We have a new hand. Mason finally got that job in Birmingham, but he sent along a buddy to replace him. Mack says he's good."

Seth nodded. "Okay. We'll be there in a second."

Jack just rolled his eyes and wandered off, leaving them alone again.

Robbie laughed. "That was close."

Seth grinned and pulled Robbie into another kiss, taking his time. Robbie's arms went around his neck, holding on tight. When they finally came up for air again, Seth rested his forehead against Robbie's.

"How ya feelin'?"

"Better." Robbie sighed. "Yesterday fucking sucked...well, until last night, anyway."

Seth smiled, swearing he saw color rising into Robbie's cheeks. He closed his eyes for a moment, remembering what it felt like. It had been ages since he'd done it to anyone, but for Robbie to allow him that...

Lord, he loved this man so much, it hurt.

"Come on," he whispered. "Let's go meet our new co-worker."

They kept a reasonable distance from each other as they headed back toward the house. Seth hated having to hide things, but until they knew this new hand, it was best to be casual. Mack's office door stood open, and Seth was just about to walk in when Robbie tugged on his arm. Mack was busy talking to the new guy, so Seth stepped back and turned around.

"Trust me," Robbie said, "this one is perfectly fine with us."

"You know him?"

Robbie snorted. "Know him? I lost my virginity to him."

Seth blinked. "Damn. Small world."

"Yeah." Robbie sighed. "Lots of baggage there."

"Want to talk to Mack about it in private?" Seth could understand the uneasiness.

"No. I'm not gonna let my past interfere in my uncle's business." Robbie smiled up at him. "I guess we gotta be the good hosts and show him his room, huh?"

"Afraid so," Seth said, wincing slightly. "You sure you're okay with him being here?"

Nodding, Robbie leaned against the wall. "Yeah, I'm cool. He's a good guy, really. We just split on..." He chewed on his bottom lip for a moment. "Not so good terms, I guess you could say."

Before Seth could reply, Mack came out, clapping the new guy on the back.

"Oh, there they are! Jeremy, meet Seth Ellis, one of the other hands, and Robbie Sexton, my nephew."

Seth tipped his hat in acknowledgement and shook Jeremy's outstretched hand. "Nice to meet you."

"Likewise." When Jeremy looked to Robbie, his expression was unreadable. "Afternoon, Robbie."

"Hey there," Robbie said quietly, shoving his hands into the pockets of his jeans.

"Well, now that we're all acquainted," Mack announced, either oblivious to the spike of tension in the air or flat-out ignoring it, "Robbie and Seth will show you where you'll be stayin'. Boys, can you do that for me? I need to return a few phone calls."

"Sure thing," Seth said with a nod. He caught the pained look from Robbie before it disappeared. "C'mon. We'll show you the guest house."

"Thanks." Jeremy fell into step behind them.

Seth just glanced at Robbie, noted the neutral expression, and decided against talking until they were alone.

Chapter Eight

Robbie kept quiet as Seth led the mini-tour of the guest house where the farmhands stayed. He couldn't believe Jeremy was here. When they passed by the bedroom he shared with Seth, Robbie ducked inside, closing the door after muttering something about needing to change clothes—anything to get him out of that situation. A few minutes later, there came a knock, then Seth's voice.

"Come in."

The door opened, and Seth walked in, closing it behind him. "Something's eatin' at you, babe." He sat down on the bed beside Robbie, one hand rubbing Robbie's back. "What's wrong?"

Robbie sighed and shook his head. "It's water under the bridge. Jeremy and I were lovers for a few years. Back then, I was too young to know what the hell I was doing. I didn't know what love really was. Then Jeremy told me he loved me."

"Okay..." Seth stretched out on the bed beside him, still petting.

"My response, in the glorious wisdom of youth, was to cheat on him. He caught us."

"Oh."

"Yeah. We didn't part on particularly good terms, and I haven't forgiven myself for it. Lord knows Jeremy probably hasn't forgiven me either."

"I take it you two haven't spoken since?"

Robbie peered up at Seth from the pillow. "Um, no."

Seth nodded and kissed his shoulder. "Then maybe it's time to get rid of those demons, Robbie. If you don't talk to him, things are gonna get so tense around here that no one will be happy."

Robbie groaned, burying his face in the pillow again. "I know," he mumbled.

Before he could say anything else, someone else knocked on the door.

"Robbie, your mama's on the phone," Ty said. "Somethin' about Kristy."

Seth got up and went to open the door. "Thanks." Then he brought the cordless over to Robbie.

Robbie rolled slightly and took the phone. "Hi, Mama."

"Hi, baby. She's awake. She and the baby are doin' good. Doctor says she can go home tomorrow. I've got your old bedroom set up for her."

"What else does she need?" Robbie asked. "For the baby, I mean? Or for herself."

Mama sighed, the sound stressed, but better than she had been at the hospital. "She's gonna need new clothes, for her and the baby when it gets here. She's not goin' back to the place she had with Russ for anything but the really important stuff. And even then, I'm goin' and with an officer."

It was wrong, so fucking wrong, for Mama to be worried enough about her safety from her own son that she had to rely on the police. Robbie growled.

"I know, baby," Mama reassured him. "It ain't right, but she's out of there now. She and the baby are safe, and in a few months, I'll be holding my first grandbaby and you'll be an uncle."

Robbie nodded. "Yeah. And if I see Russ again, I'll kill him."

"No, you won't, Robert Sexton. You're a good man; don't let this change you. You see Russ, you ignore him. If he comes around, I'll call the police. But don't you lay a finger on him. I don't want you in jail because of this."

"Yes, Mama." Robbie sighed, elbowing Seth when the cowboy chuckled softly.

"I need to go, baby. I'll call you when we get home. Love you."

"Love you, too, Mama." Robbie pushed the 'off' button and handed the phone to Seth, who set it on the bedside table.

"Well?"

"Kristy's going home tomorrow. She's gonna need some stuff, or Mama needs some extra money for some stuff for Kristy and the baby. Oh, and I've been forbidden from even so much as looking at my brother if he comes around."

Seth snorted. "Smart woman."

"Shut up."

Seth laughed and kissed Robbie's head. "Love you."

Robbie rolled over and smiled. "Love you, too."

"We can make it through this."

Robbie nodded. "I know. If there's anything in this world I don't have doubts about, it's us."

"Good."

* * *

"Never, in a million years, did I expect to see you again."

Robbie stopped just as he reached for the wire cutters. Closing his eyes, he took a deep breath. "Hi, Jeremy."

"Thought you were up in Baltimore."

Turning his head, Robbie glanced up at his former lover. "I was. How'd you know that?"

Jeremy shrugged and leaned back against the wall of the chicken coop Robbie had been repairing. "Hearsay. Stopped off at the Seven Nations parlor a few times, shopping for ink."

Robbie nodded, turned back to his work. "New ink, huh? Anything good?" He reached back blindly for the wire cutters, only to have them handed to him. "Thanks."

"Yeah, I'm happy with him. Rogue did the work. Didn't know it 'til after he'd started that it was one of yours."

That got his attention, and Robbie nearly cut the wrong damned bit of chicken wire. "Mine?"

"Yeah. The fallen angel. Wanna see him?"

Robbie started to ask where the tat was, but before he could, he heard Jeremy moving. He turned and watched as Jeremy lifted his shirt up, back to him. There, on the man's right shoulder blade, was his favorite piece he'd ever done. Robbie wasn't sure if he was proud of how good it looked, or if the slight nausea that started was something other than the heat outside.

"Looks good," he said finally.

Jeremy sighed and let the shirt fall back down. "Robbie..."

"Look..." Robbie dropped the wire cutters into the toolbox. "I'm sorry, Jeremy. I know what I did can't be excused, but please believe me when I say that I'm sorry for hurting you."

Wandering over to the fence, Jeremy leaned on the railing and looked out at the pasture where the cows were grazing. "I loved you."

Robbie winced. Fuck, that stung. "I know."

"But you know what? I forgave you. We were both young, didn't really know what we were doing."

Robbie stood beside him. "Yeah, we were."

"So, this new man. You love him?"

The question caught him off-guard, and Robbie stared at Jeremy. "How did—"

Jeremy laughed. "C'mon, Robbie. It would take an idiot to not see how you two look at each other."

"Oh. Yeah, I guess so."

"Promise me something?" Jeremy turned to face him, hip cocked against the fence, arms crossed.

"What?"

Jeremy smiled, the expression genuine. "Love him with everything you are, Robbie. He seems like a good man. We both fucked up back then, but we've grown up, moved on."

"I do love him. Friends?" He extended a hand to Jeremy but was surprised when he was pulled into a tight hug.

"Friends."

"Robbie!"

"Yeah?" Robbie looked toward the main house where Mack stood on the front porch, cordless phone in his hand. "Coming!" He patted Jeremy on the shoulder and headed up to the house, taking the phone from Mack. "Hello?"

"Hi, baby!"

"Hi, Mama. How's Kristy?" He walked across the porch and leaned against the railing.

"She's good. We're home now."

Robbie heard a door close quietly, then she continued.

"She's..." Mama sniffled. "She's talkin' about giving up the baby."

"What? Why?"

Mama sighed. "She's afraid she won't have the money to care for it now. Russ was bringin' in the money, what little there was. I mean, she and the baby are under Medicaid right now, and the baby will stay on it once it's born, but Kristy won't be able to work and care for a baby, too."

Robbie closed his eyes, fought back the anger at Russ, and swallowed the pain. "Will you let me give you some money to help 'til the baby's born?"

"Baby, I can't..."

"Mama, please. It's not fair to you to shoulder the expenses, and it's not Kristy's fault that she was abandoned. I want to help. Please?"

There was a good bit of silence, and Robbie began to wonder if she'd keep arguing. Then she finally let out a long exhale.

"All right."

"Good. What do you need right now? I don't know a damn thing about babies."

Mama chuckled. "You wantin' a list?"

"Sure. You got one? Does Kristy have one of those baby registry things somewhere?"

"Actually, hold on a sec." The sound of her rummaging through a drawer followed, and then she came back. "Yeah, here it is. She's registered at JC Penney, under Kristy Sexton."

"Wishful thinking, huh?"

"I think so. She's doing good, though. She's madder than a rattlesnake, so she'll be okay."

"Cool. Now tell me what she needs or wants."

Robbie spent the next twenty minutes listening to Mama rattle off a list of general items: blankets, bottles, sheets, a crib, clothes; whatever babies needed. He made a mental note of some things, said his goodbyes, and hung up. He'd need to sell some flash to cover the crib, but everything else was pretty much covered by savings. He took the phone back into the house and hung it up in the kitchen. Then he went searching for a newspaper. For what he had in mind, it'd take a new place to live.

Finding a newspaper, he grabbed it and headed back to the guest house. He got a Coke from the fridge and settled down at the table, flipping to the want ads. He heard the front door close a few minutes later.

"Apartments for rent. You leaving?"

He stopped reading and pushed his chair back. Twisting, he tugged Seth to him, the cowboy straddling his lap. "Not leaving you, babe."

"But..."

"Mama called." Robbie looked up into those green eyes. "She said Kristy was thinking about giving the baby up, something about not having money to pay for everything."

"Oh, damn."

"Yeah." Robbie rested his forehead on Seth's chest.

"Don't tell me you're thinkin' about adoption." Seth chuckled. Robbie whacked him on the thigh. Hard. "Ow!"

"Smartass."

"Okay, okay. Seriously, what's with the ads for apartments?"

"Well..." Robbie glanced over at the newspaper on the kitchen table. "Was thinkin' maybe we could find a place close, one with two or three bedrooms." He didn't look up, didn't have to; a finger under his chin tilted his head up.

"Mack was right," Seth said quietly.

"About what?"

Those eyes sparkled, reflecting Seth's smile. "You're a good man, Robbie Sexton."

Robbie smiled slowly just before his lips were captured, the kiss soft. He slid his arms around his cowboy's waist, about the same time 'I love you' was breathed into him.

"You find anything?" Seth asked, lips moving over his jaw.

Robbie tipped his head. "Huh?"

"Apartments, baby."

"Oh!"

Seth chuckled and nipped his throat. Robbie shivered.

"Um, y-yeah..." He groaned. "Fuck. Seth."

"Should I stop?"

"Fuck, no." Robbie let his hands slip down to cup that tight, denim-covered ass.

"Keep talkin'."

Robbie's eyes rolled back when the light nibbles turned to outright bites. His hips jerked.

"Want my nipple pierced."

Robbie croaked out, "W-what?"

"Want my nipple pierced," Seth repeated with a soft chuckle.

Robbie pushed a hand up under Seth's shirt and gave his cowboy's left nipple a sharp twist. Seth grunted. "You serious?"

"Yeah."

One eyebrow rose. "Out of sheer curiosity, what gave you the idea?"

Seth grinned and kissed him, then stood up. "I know how sensitive yours is, and after thinking about it for a bit, I decided I wanted one." He shrugged. "Call me nuts."

"You're nuts." Robbie looked up at his cowboy. "But you sure as shit won't hear me complain."

"I'm assuming you know a good, safe place?"

Robbie nodded and stood as well. "Seven Nations in Huntsville. I used to work there."

"Cool. Now let's go play in the shower."

Chapter Nine

"Well, I'll be damned. Robert fucking Sexton."

Robbie laughed, letting the shop door close behind them. "Long time, no see." He shook Archie Mathis' hand, then turned to Seth. "Archie, this is Seth Ellis. Seth, this is Archie Mathis, owner of Seven Nations Tattoos."

"Howdy," Seth said with a grin. "Fine shop you have here."

"Thank you, thank you." Archie beamed, the man's joy and pride contagious. "So, y'all together?"

Smiling, Robbie glanced at Seth. "Very much so."

Archie snorted. "Lord, boy, you're smitten. What can I do for ya?"

Seth grinned and took off his hat, raking his fingers through his hair. "I've decided to get my nipple pierced."

Archie nodded and reached behind the counter for the consent forms. "Know which one yet?" He ripped off a sheet and handed it to Seth, along with a pen.

"No clue." Leaning against the countertop to fill out the form, Seth looked over his shoulder briefly. "Robbie?"

Robbie blinked, tore his gaze from an ass so tight he swore he could bounce a quarter off of it. "Uhh...left?"

Seth winked and flashed him a grin, then turned back to the form. Once he was done, Archie took the form and put it in the file cabinet behind the counter.

"All right, let's go!" Archie clapped his hands, rubbing them together like a mad scientist.

As they followed him down the short hall to one of the rooms, Seth muttered, "I'm never gonna live this down."

Clearing his throat, Robbie fought like hell to bite back the chuckle. "Nope."

"Just have a seat and take off your shirt," Archie said as he pulled the black curtain across the doorway.

Crossing his arms, Seth tugged his shirt over his head, then handed it to Robbie. Robbie draped the shirt over his arm and watched Archie putter around, setting out the tools on a paper towel-lined tray. Archie reclined Seth's chair a little bit and pulled the tray over beside him.

"Okay, this is just alcohol."

Archie rubbed Seth's left nipple with an alcohol-soaked cotton ball. The little nub stood at attention, drawn tight. Robbie resisted the urge to lick his lips. He shivered and remained plastered against the wall, gaze riveted to that bit of flesh as Archie set the clamp on it. Seth's hands tightened on the arms of the chair with the tug of the clamp.

"Just breathe for me," Archie said. "One, two, three..."

"Fuck!" Seth's hips jerked the second the needle pierced his flesh.

Robbie's knees nearly gave way, the room spinning slightly. Seth panted and hissed through his teeth when Archie slid the ring through the hole.

"No playing with it for eight weeks," Archie instructed. He took away the clamp and set the bead in place, tightening the ring. "Clean it twice a day for the next three to four days, using fresh, clean water. No soap or shampoo or anything like that. Use a high-quality, anti-bacterial soap and be sure to rotate the ring during cleaning and when rinsing."

"Looks..." Robbie shifted, tried to will away the terminal hard-on. "Damn fucking hot," he said quietly.

"No Neosporin or the like," Archie continued. "After the first three or four days, you only need to clean it once a day as instructed." He stepped back and grinned. "All of this is on the After-Care Instructions sheet I'll give you up front."

Seth looked down at his newly-skewered nipple, then up—past Archie—and right at Robbie. "Thanks, man."

Archie chuckled. "Come on up front when you're ready."

Once they were alone, Robbie found himself flattened against the wall, Seth's tongue down his throat. He hadn't even registered the man moving, but damned if he could miss that hard-as-diamond cock pressing against his own through denim and cotton. Seth made sure to keep the left side of his chest back a little, but those rough hands worked up under Robbie's shirt, making him forget he even had a name.

"Home," Robbie panted for a brief second when they came up for air.

Seth kissed him again, hard and deep, then stepped back. He put his shirt back on slowly and opened the curtain. Robbie nodded and left the room, Seth right behind him, gaze moving over him like a caress. After paying and thanking Archie, they hurried out to the truck. Robbie almost had his hand on the door handle when a hand wrapped tight in his hair, jerking his head back. Seth's mouth latched onto the side of his throat, hot and determined. Sparks shot up Robbie's spine, and the pain made a beeline for his cock.

"Seth. Please." His eyes rolled back when Seth bit down.

Seth whispered. "I have plans for you tonight. I want you naked and spread out for me."

Swallowing hard, Robbie opened the truck door after Seth released him. "Any-fucking-thing."

* * *

To say he was a fish out of water was an understatement. Hell, judging by the blank look on Robbie's face, Seth was pretty damned sure he wasn't alone. The sweet, young salesperson remained patient, though, asking only the easy questions once she realized that here were two gay men who didn't know the first damned thing about shopping.

"Okay, any idea what the baby is yet?"

Robbie shook his head. "Not yet. I guess we need gender-neutral type stuff."

The amused but patient Julie smiled and nodded. "We can work with that." She led them further into the baby section of JC Penney. "She have a baby registry account?" She stopped at a computer terminal and started speed-typing as Robbie spelled out the name. "Here she is! This makes things so much easier."

Seth moved up to stand behind Robbie, arms sliding around Robbie's waist as he peered over his lover's shoulder. Julie scrolled through the four pages of baby items that Kristy had picked out, only one or two of which had been bought. He knew Robbie's Mama didn't have the money to be shellin' out for this stuff, and it wasn't fair for her to do it anyhow, seeing as how she'd raised two boys herself.

"How much are the basics all together? The crib, the car seat, the mattress, and the sheets," Seth asked, chin resting lightly on Robbie's shoulder.

Julie checked off the items, then hit the total button. "Roughly four hundred and ten dollars."

"Ouch," Robbie muttered.

Seth chuckled softly, then patted Robbie's hip. "Didn't you see a diaper bag you thought she'd like?"

"Yeah."

"Good. Let's start with that. Can you go get it?"

Robbie turned his head, one eyebrow raised. "Okay…"

Soon as Robbie was out of ear-shot, Seth pulled his wallet out. "Pay for it now before he comes back." He grinned and handed Julie his Visa card.

She laughed and rang up the basics, swiped his card, and had his signature all before Robbie returned, pink camo diaper bag in hand. Thankfully, the delivery instructions had already been changed to Robbie's Mama's house in the registry.

"It just screams Kristy," Robbie said.

"Cool. Okay, Julie, we'll take this."

Seth was grateful Julie was the type who could keep from giggling at a secret. She rang up the diaper bag for them and handed Seth the receipt, conveniently slipping the previous one into his hand as well.

"Thank you, ma'am." He tipped his hat and gave her a quick, discreet wink.

"Thank you," she said, beaming a smile.

"Come on, love," Seth said, draping an arm around Robbie's shoulders. "Let's get to your Mama's and check on things."

"You're hiding something."

How the hell he kept a…well, 'straight' face, Seth had no idea. "Hidin' somethin'?" He gave Robbie his best 'who, me?' look.

Robbie just rolled his eyes. "Fine, don't tell me. But see if I tell you what you're getting for Christmas from Mama."

"That's still a little over four months away."

They got to the truck, and Robbie climbed in, sticking his tongue out. "Asshole."

Grinning, Seth closed the door and went around. As he got in and buckled, he said, "I can think of things to do with assholes and tongues..." He started the truck up. "...and they have *nothin'* to do with babies or Christmas."

Those blue eyes went dark, Robbie licking his lips. "Oh, yeah?"

"Yeah." Seth pulled out of the parking lot.

They both fell silent on the way home, and Seth thought back to the times when he'd wanted to explore other things with Robbie, things he wasn't sure his lover would be interested in. Though, judging by the way Robbie's breath had hitched when Seth pulled his hair earlier in the day, maybe that wouldn't be an issue. Tension and need radiated between them. When he glanced at Robbie, he found himself the sole focus of a gaze hotter than hell.

"Robbie?"

The button popped on Robbie's jeans.

"Babe."

"Take the back way."

Seth just nodded, saying a silent prayer he wouldn't put them in the ditch. He heard Robbie shift, heard the sound of skin sliding on skin, and risked another look. Oh, fuck him. He looked back to the road, cock jerking and pushing against his jeans, and groaned when he heard Robbie's breath catch.

"Fuck..." The word was whispered, Robbie sounding needy and desperate. "Seth..."

Shifting on the bench seat, Seth gritted his teeth, hands tightening on the steering wheel.

"Wanna feel you," Robbie said, voice deep, rough, laced with want. "Want your cock deep inside me, Seth." He moaned softly. "Please..."

That was it. Seth started looking for a good place to pull over, somewhere off the road, out of sight. He needed Robbie in the worst way and couldn't wait any longer. Finding a heavily-wooded road, he took it, going only God-knew-where and not caring in the least. Satisfied they wouldn't be seen, he stopped the truck and set the emergency brake. Robbie wasted no time in stripping off his jeans. Then Seth had his lap and hands full of hot, horny male.

"Fuck me," Robbie panted. "Please, Seth, fuck me hard. Here. Now."

Seth managed to scoot over to the passenger's side. "Lube. Glove compartment." He'd learned to keep the stuff handy. As Robbie twisted slightly, Seth latched onto the nearest bit of flesh: Robbie's right nipple.

"Seth!" Robbie jerked, snapped the glove compartment shut. "Now."

Without relinquishing the nipple in his mouth, Seth held up his right hand. Once his fingers were slick, Robbie guided them down and back, body going tight as Seth pushed both fingers deep inside that sweet, hot ass. He worked them in and out, cock throbbing, Robbie getting his jeans open. Soon as he was freed, he pulled his fingers out and lined up, hands tight on Robbie's hips as he slid on home.

"Oh, fuck." Seth's head fell back, a deep shudder rolling through him as Robbie's mouth moved over his throat, breath warming him.

"Come on, baby," Robbie whispered. "Fuck me."

Raising his head, Seth gripped Robbie's hip in one hand and cupped the back of Robbie's head with the other. Diving into a deep, hungry kiss, he started thrusting hard, cock piercing Robbie's body over and over. Robbie fed him moans and gasps, riding and bouncing on his prick, pushing them both closer to the edge.

"Don't stop, don't stop," Robbie chanted. "Oh. Fuck. Seth!"

Seth gasped, Robbie's ass clamping around him hard enough to take his breath away. Heat shot between them, soaking their shirts, and then he was following, growling as he filled Robbie with his load. Fighting to catch his breath, he held on tight and smiled when Robbie let out a contented sound.

"Better?"

Robbie nuzzled his neck. "Much better, babe. Love you."

Seth chuckled and kissed the disheveled brown hair spilling over both of them. "Love you, too." He held on, eyes closed, loving the way Robbie felt against him, around him. Only when he went soft and slipped out did he even think about moving.

"Need to be gettin' to your mama's, baby."

Groaning, Robbie nodded. "Guess that requires movement, huh?"

"Afraid so."

Robbie grumbled, but rose up just enough for Seth to scoot over. Using a rag from a box behind the bench seat, they both cleaned up. Once they were tucked in and buckled, Seth stole a quick kiss and got them back on the road toward Athens.

What had started out as a nice day ended up dark and stormy by the time they reached Mama's. The front door opened just as they pulled up to the house, Mama shaking her head and laughing at them. Robbie was out first, JC Penney bag in his hand, and ran to the door. Seth just barely made it to the porch before the sky opened up and dumped a year's worth of rain in less than a few minutes.

"Lord, Lord." Mama chuckled, eyeing the bag as she held the door open for them. "What did you two get?"

Seth took off his hat and stood to the side while Robbie hugged Mama. "Oh, just a little something for Kristy, ma'am."

Mama glared at him and gave his arm a rather weighty smack, then pulled him into a tight hug. "You call me 'ma'am' again, and I'll beat you to death, Seth Ellis. Call me 'Mama.'"

Robbie snorted and ducked out of the way before Seth could swat him. "Yes, ma'am—Mama."

"That's a good boy." She stepped back and grinned. "C'mon, Kristy's in her bedroom, putting together a baby book."

"Robbie!"

Seth rounded the doorway with Mama just in time to see Kristy throwing her arms around Robbie's neck as he leaned over the bed. Robbie laughed and sat down on the bed beside her before pulling her into another hug.

"Hi there, sweetie."

Kristy finally released him and flopped back down onto the bed. The bandage on her head was gone, though her eye was still slightly swollen. The bruise had turned to dark yellow, and there were a few stitches here and there on her face. Still, Kristy looked none the worse for wear. For that matter, she looked stronger.

"Seth!" She reached out, and Seth bent, giving her a gentle hug. "Oh, I didn't know you were coming, too. Y'all finally out?"

Glancing at Robbie, Seth just laughed. "More or less. How ya doin', kiddo?"

Kristy shrugged. "Not bad. Tired of being in the damn bed."

Mama cleared her throat, and Kristy blushed, ducking her head. "I'm gonna leave y'all to chat. Robbie, Seth: you thirsty?"

"Coke if you got it, Mama," Robbie answered. "Babe?"

"Same. I'll help you." Seth patted Kristy's leg and stood to follow Mama into the kitchen.

Soon as they were out of earshot of the bedroom, Mama turned to him and surprised Seth by giving him a tight, tight hug. "Oh, thank you, Seth," she whispered. "I know it was you who bought the stuff. They just called to confirm delivery."

Seth smiled. "You're more than welcome."

Mama pulled back, teary-eyed and sniffling a little. "You're a beautiful man, Seth Ellis. My baby did good." She reached up and patted Seth's cheek. "C'mon, let's get those drinks."

Two glasses of ice-cold Coke in hand, Seth went back into Kristy's bedroom. Robbie was lying on the queen-sized bed beside her, both of them looking through the in-progress baby book. The JC Penney bag sat on the floor on Robbie's side of the bed. Seth set their drinks on the bedside table and pulled up the rocking chair.

"Hey, baby." Robbie looked up and grinned. "You oughta see this thing," he said, pointing to the book.

"Yeah?" Seth leaned over. "Oh, nice," he said when Kristy twisted the book to show him.

"Thanks. Mama's been helpin' me put it together. Wanna show ya both somethin'." She flipped through to the beginning, stopping at the family tree page. Starting at the top, she read out each name, beginning with the blank space for the baby's. When she got to the father's family side, her finger rested on the 'aunt' and 'uncle' spaces. 'Aunt' had been whited out; 'uncle' written in its place.

"Damn."

Seth just nodded, silently echoing Robbie.

"Thought y'all might like that," Kristy said quietly. "This baby's gonna grow up to know there's no difference."

"Love you, sweetie," Robbie said, kissing Kristy's forehead. "This baby will drown in love, too."

Seth looked up at them both and smiled. "Sure is. Being a part of this family would bless anyone."

Chapter Ten

"Guess you know all about Russ?"

As he closed the refrigerator door, Seth nodded. He handed one of the beers to Jeremy and motioned toward the living room. "Yeah. First introductions were interesting, guess you could say."

They went the living room, settling on opposite ends of the couch, somewhat facing each other. Seth glanced up at the clock on top of the entertainment center. Robbie would be home from Mama's soon. Two days ago, Kristy had been itching to get out of bed when they'd visited. Robbie went today to help her along a little while Mama ran a few errands.

"Russ was always trouble."

"Just hard to believe that he came from such good people," Seth mused.

"You mean Robbie didn't tell you?"

Seth looked up, blinked. "Tell me what?"

For a moment, Jeremy looked like a deer caught in headlights. "Susan and Gerald Sexton adopted Russ at the age of two months. Robbie was ten."

Beer forgotten, Seth just shook his head. "No, he didn't tell me. Guess that explains the lack of love there."

"Pretty much," Jeremy said, taking a sip of his own beer. "So what about you? I've not had much of a chance to get details from Robbie."

"Me?"

"Yeah. Where are you from? Brothers? Sisters? That sort of thing."

"Oh." Seth stared at his bottle and began picking at the label. "Well, I'm thirty-four, born and raised in Taylor, Texas. Only child; mom died six years ago. I left Texas shortly after."

"What about your dad?" Jeremy asked. "I'm sorry. It's none of my business."

"No, no. It's okay." Seth gave him a slight smile. "Dad didn't take too kindly to having, as he put it, 'a faggot in the family.'"

Silence reigned for a moment, then Jeremy said, "I'm sorry. Really."

Seth shrugged and took a drink. "No love lost. We never got along."

They fell into a companionable silence until Jeremy announced he was heading to bed about fifteen minutes later. With a pat on Seth's shoulder, Jeremy left the living room. Seth stared at the blank TV screen for another fifteen minutes, gaze occasionally wandering to the cordless phone on the coffee table. Another ten minutes passed while a tug war played out in his head. He finally pulled a crumpled piece of paper from his wallet. Taking a deep breath, he dialed the number.

"Hello?"

"Hi, Dad."

The line went dead.

No love lost, Seth.

"Seth?"

"In the living room."

"Hey, babe. Sorry I'm..." Robbie stepped around the couch and crouched down in front of him. "What's wrong?"

Seth shook his head and let it fall back against the couch. "Nothin', babe. Just tired." He looked down at Robbie, who gazed at the phone still in Seth's hand. "Yeah, I tried. Pointless, but I tried."

"Damn." Robbie took the phone, set it on the table, and sat on the couch beside Seth, facing him. "Wanna talk about it?"

"Not really. Nothing to tell. I said hi; he hung up."

"It's amazing how family can cut so deep."

Seth rolled his head to the side. "Why didn't you tell me about Russ?"

Sighing, Robbie stared down at the cushions, finding them utterly fascinating all of a sudden. "Guess I didn't want to think about it," he said quietly. "Mama and Dad adopted him when I was ten. He was only about two months old. They couldn't have more kids because Mama had trouble after I was born and ended up having a hysterectomy. I tried, I really did."

"Was he always like he is now?"

Robbie shook his head and scooted close, just cuddling. "No. He didn't get bad until he hit puberty. Hormones went fucking crazy then. They tried putting him on medication for depression and mood swings, but he never took it."

"Did they ever find out what might have been behind it? Or was it just a random chemical imbalance thing?"

"We thought it was a random thing, just a teenage boy's hormones way out of whack. Things really got bad when he was sixteen. That's when they told him he was adopted. He was pissed off at Dad from then on out."

Seth wrapped his arm around Robbie and kissed his hair. "What about your Mama?"

"I think Russ is ambivalent toward her. It's me he hates, though. We never got along, always felt like a constant competition in everything we did."

"How did he find out you were gay?"

Robbie groaned and burrowed closer, arm sliding around Seth's waist. "He saw me kissing Jeremy."

"Oh. Yeah, I guess that was a shocker."

"You ain't kiddin'. It was the first physical fight Russ and I got into. Thank God Mama wasn't at home. Not sure what the hell kept him from telling her."

Seth growled, remembering the fight he'd broken up at Robbie's Dad's wake. "Well, sure doesn't matter anymore."

"Nope. Oh, speaking of Mama…" Robbie sat up. "She needs us to help move some stuff tomorrow. Someone bought Kristy some baby furniture."

"Cool!" Seth was proud of himself; his mouth didn't even twitch. "What time?"

"The guy from JC Penney told her they'd deliver it around noon."

He nodded and fought the urge to grin. "That works. Does Mack know?"

"Yep. We have the rest of the night and all day tomorrow and tomorrow night off." Robbie grinned slowly.

"Whatever will we do to pass the time?"

"Oh…"

A finger traced just around Seth's left nipple, and he shifted slightly, the sensations sharp thanks to the piercing. Robbie leaned in and licked just below his ear.

"I'm sure we could think of something."

"Upstairs," Seth rumbled. "Now."

Robbie slid off the couch and started for the doorway. "Coming?"

Seth watched that sweet ass walk away. "I will be," he said as he got up.

"Mmm, promise?" Robbie went up the steps, ass moving in those tight jeans.

Licking his lips, Seth just nodded. "Uh-huh."

He followed Robbie into their bedroom and closed the door, locking it. Robbie went to the bed and pulled his shirt off. Seth leaned back against the door, thumbs hooked in the waistband of his jeans.

"You're not undressing," Robbie said as he popped the button on his jeans.

"Watching." And watch Seth did, gaze riveted as that beautiful body was slowly revealed to him. "Fuck, you're hot."

Robbie kicked off his boots and jeans, and then started toward him. "Want you."

Seth nodded, drinking in the sight. "Got me."

"Inside me."

"In every way possible."

Soon as Robbie was within reach, Seth caught a wrist, jerking Robbie up against him. Robbie groaned, pushing closer. He wrapped his other hand in Robbie's long hair and tugged. Robbie hissed, cock flexing against Seth's still-clothed body.

"Want to feel you everywhere, Seth."

Seth bent and bit down on the side of Robbie's neck, shivering as his lover cried out. Pulling away, he said, "Shower. Want to get slick and taste."

"Fuck yes."

Soon as Seth let go, Robbie stepped back and went into the bathroom to start the water while Seth undressed. Once it was going, they both stepped in, Seth crowding Robbie up against the wall. The water was just on the hot side, spraying down over them as he moved Robbie's hair to the side, kissing a path over the slick skin. Robbie's fingers curled to his hip, holding Seth against that ass.

"Seth..." Robbie groaned and turned his head, meeting Seth in a kiss.

Seth slipped a hand between them and lifted Robbie's leg. With Robbie's foot propped on the little ledge, Seth had just enough access to play. Plundering Robbie's mouth with his tongue, he swallowed the moan as he slid a finger into that tight hole.

Robbie shuddered and bore down, driving Seth's finger deeper. The fingers on Seth's hip tightened, digging into his skin. He broke the kiss and slowly moved down Robbie's spine, finger still buried inside. As he neared Robbie's ass, he started nipping the skin, loving the gasps, the way Robbie's hole clamped down on his finger.

"Fuck...Seth..." Robbie shifted and rose up a little on his foot, pushing his ass out and down. "More."

Seth settled on his knees and finally pulled his finger out. Gripping Robbie's ass cheeks, he spread them apart, mouth watering. "Hell, yes."

He leaned in and flicked his tongue over Robbie's hole, growling when a moan met his ears. This wasn't the best position to do what he wanted, but he made do, tilting Robbie's hips at just the right angle. Then he dove in, pushing his tongue as deep inside Robbie's ass as he could.

"Oh, fuck..." Robbie gasped and groaned, thighs shaking. "Don't stop. Oh, fuck, don't stop."

Seth had absolutely no intention of stopping. He held Robbie wide open, feasting, drowning in the taste of his lover's body. He could smell Robbie's arousal—musky and sharp. He opened Robbie even more and plunged his tongue in and out. Robbie shook in his hands, words completely degenerating into moans and grunts, hips moving, pushing back. Seth was hard as a rock, cock aching and balls tight. He reached around with one hand and wrapped his fingers around Robbie's prick. Robbie's hips jerked suddenly.

Seth's name started raining down over him, mixing with the water and the steam. He twisted them both slightly, never letting go of Robbie's prick, until Robbie was bent over, hands braced on the back of the tub. The position afforded him more leverage, and Seth took full advantage, sucking on the puckered hole before thrusting his tongue back inside. Robbie's hand joined his, both of them stroking.

"Seth...gonna come..." Robbie panted. "Oh...fuck!"

Robbie's ass clenched around Seth's tongue, and heat spilled over their fingers. He didn't give Robbie a chance to catch his breath, just stood quickly and thrust his cock into that hot ass, free hand grabbing Robbie's hip.

"Yes!" Robbie's other hand went to the tub rim, and he rocked back, meeting Seth's thrusts. "Come on, babe. Fuck me."

Seth didn't last much longer, giving Robbie's ass several hard thrusts, both of them riding the burn. Burying himself deep inside, he grunted, filling that gorgeous body. Breathless and boneless, he leaned down, resting his forehead on Robbie's back.

"Damn." Robbie panted and reached back to pat Seth's hip. "Bed, babe. Need to get horizontal."

Laughing, Seth slipped out. "Good idea. This position only works for so long."

Once they were rinsed, they got out and dried. Seth crawled into bed and waited, holding the covers up for Robbie to slide in with him. Gathering Robbie close, he leaned down for a kiss.

"Love you," he whispered.

"Love you, too, baby." Robbie snuggled against him, smiling contentedly.

* * *

"Mama, the truck's here," Robbie called out. He propped the screen door open and headed out to meet the two men who'd come to deliver the baby stuff. Before he could say a word, however, a single question from one of the men stopped him cold.

"Mr. Ellis?"

Robbie blinked. "Huh?"

The guy looked at the clipboard in his hand. "Yeah, Mr. Seth Ellis," the guy said. "Just need him—or whoever—to sign."

Nodding, Robbie took the pen and clipboard. There—in barely legible chicken scratch—was his cowboy's name. It wasn't Seth's handwriting, but it sure as hell was his name and, below it, Seth's cell phone number.

"I don't know what to do first: kick his ass, or kiss him," Robbie muttered as he signed Seth's name. He handed the clipboard back to the delivery guy, not missing the odd look he got, but not giving a damn either.

"Thanks," the guy said. "We'll just...uh...get this stuff inside for ya."

Robbie hung back while the guys unloaded the stuff. When he realized what all they'd brought, his mind flashed back to that day in JC Penney. Seth had asked the saleslady how much the basics were, then sent Robbie for a damned diaper bag.

"Seth Ellis!"

Turning on his heel, Robbie went back inside, heading right for Kristy's room where Seth was busy rearranging things to make room. Robbie waited until Seth was done, then grabbed one broad shoulder and spun his lover around, giving Seth's other arm a good whack.

"You are the sneakiest, most..." Seth's unabashed grin undid Robbie before he could really get going. "...wonderful man I've ever fucking known." Then he proceeded to kiss his lover dizzy, swallowing Seth's laughter in the process.

Seth's arms went around him, holding Robbie close. "You're welcome."

"Why didn't you tell me?"

"Because it was more fun to surprise you." Seth leaned in for another kiss, this one softer. "Besides, every time I felt like I couldn't hold it back anymore, you'd make me forget."

"Mmm...really?"

Seth nodded, tongue sliding across Robbie's lips. "Oh, yeah."

"Lord, y'all are hopeless."

Robbie nearly jumped out of his skin, which only made Seth and Kristy burst into laughter. "Oh, yes...fun at my expense." He held out a hand to Kristy. "How ya feeling?"

She let Robbie pull her into a hug. "I'm good. Still stiff, and the headaches are a bitch, but at least my face doesn't look like I got into a paint fight. God, those bruises were fucking awful."

"Shh," Seth whispered. "Don't want Mama to hear you talkin' like that in her house."

Kristy rolled her eyes dramatically. "Oh, believe me. I've slipped up enough for the three of us combined, and I've been here less than a week."

Robbie twisted until his back was to Seth, those strong arms closing around him again. "I love her to death, but she's not easy to live with sometimes."

"Ugh, tell me about it. I mean, I'm beyond grateful. She sure doesn't have to do this, but...yeah."

Robbie nodded. "Trust me, I know."

Mama's voice filled the hallway, and a few minutes later, the delivery men carried in the big box that was obviously the crib. Mama carried in a shopping bag behind them and set it on Kristy's bed.

"You want us to put it together?" one of the guys asked.

"No, no, hun. Just bring it all in. My son and son-in-law will do the rest." Mama flashed Robbie, who just kinda stood there with his mouth hanging open, a grin and left the room.

"Son-in-law?" Kristy asked.

Robbie shook his head. "Lord, you'd think we were getting married or something."

Seth kissed the curve of Robbie's ear and whispered, "She's a mama: hopeful and determined."

Kristy patted her growing belly. "I've already got the grandkid thing covered. Guess you boys oughta start the wedding planning." She squealed and left the room before Robbie could go after her.

He laughed. "What in Heaven's name has gotten into everyone?"

"Like I said: hopeful." Seth nipped his ear, nodding slightly when the delivery guys brought in the mattress and the car seat box. "Thanks, guys. We'll take it from here."

Both men waved and seemed to make a quick beeline down the hall.

Robbie snorted and shook his head. "Heaven forbid they should see two men together."

"The South isn't known for its progressiveness," Seth said. "C'mon. You hungry?"

"Yeah. I'm craving the hell out of a good, thick steak."

Seth turned Robbie around and grinned. "That all you're craving that's thick?"

"Oh, fuck no." Taking a quick peek at the door, Robbie slipped a hand between them and cupped Seth through his jeans. "If I wasn't actually hungry for food, I'd be begging for something else entirely."

"Mmm..." Seth hummed, hips pushing forward, pressing harder against Robbie's fingers. "Let's go eat, and then we'll see what we can do about your other cravings."

Robbie laughed. "Deal."

They met Mama and Kristy in the living room. The delivery truck was just pulling out of the driveway.

"Y'all hungry?" Seth asked as he picked up his hat off the coffee table. "We were thinkin' about steak."

"Oh, steak." Kristy groaned and nudged Mama with her elbow. "You up for it, Mama?"

Mama slid her purse strap over her shoulder. "I'm always game for a nice steak. There's a new Lonestar opened up off 72."

"Then let's go!" Robbie kissed Mama's cheek, whispering, "our treat, Mama."

"You sure, baby?"

"Absolutely." He patted her shoulder and joined Seth at the front door. "We'll meet you there. Whoever gets there first gets the table."

Robbie followed Seth out to the truck, and a few minutes later, Mama and Kristy walked out of the house.

"You still thinkin' about finding a place for all of us?" Seth asked, backing out of the driveway.

"Yeah." Robbie glanced over at him. "You cool with it?"

Seth smiled and put the truck in first gear, then started down the road. "You know it. Besides, who's gonna warm my bed if you're gone?"

Robbie reached across the bench seat and traced a line up Seth's thigh with his fingertip. "No one's warming your bed but me, Cowboy."

The look that Seth shot him was hot as hell. "You got that right."

By the time they pulled into the Lonestar Steakhouse parking lot, Robbie's prick was arguing with his stomach. He was hard as a rock, with a growling stomach to boot. He grumbled about damned sexy Texans under his breath and unbuckled, but before he could open the door, one big hand grabbed his arm and hauled him across the seat. It took all he had not to crawl into Seth's lap right then and there as his cowboy's tongue pushed into his mouth, the kiss hard and promising much more to come later. When Seth finally let him up for air, Robbie was practically dizzy.

"Fuck."

"Yep." Seth unbuckled and adjusted his prick in his jeans. "We get done here, and that's the idea."

Robbie groaned and shifted his cock slightly so the zipper wasn't pressing into it. "Okay. Food. Then fucking."

They were still laughing when they opened the restaurant door, Seth holding it for a group of young women who all but tripped over themselves while staring at him and giggling. Robbie made a point to get himself a handful of genuine Texan ass in plain sight, just in case it wasn't clear who this particular Texan was going home with tonight.

Chapter Eleven

Mama sighed, though she tried to hide it. "I don't see why you should have to do this."

Robbie switched the phone to his other ear and took the offered plate from Seth. "I know I don't *have* to do it, Mama, but I want to." He gave his cowboy a smile, mouthing 'thank you' as Seth sat down across the table from him.

"Robbie." Mama paused. "Are you sure?"

Spearing one of the roasted red potatoes, Robbie blew on it to cool it off. "Yes, I'm sure. We both are." He popped the potato in his mouth and hummed appreciatively. If anything, he sure as hell wouldn't starve with Seth's cooking. Seth's barbeque and red potatoes beat the steak they'd had at Lonestar the night before.

"All right," Mama conceded. "Want me to tell her now? Or wait 'til you've got a place?"

"Up to you. We found some promising places in the paper."

"Okay, baby. I'll let her know. Love you, Robbie. And Seth."

Robbie smiled, glancing up to meet his cowboy's gaze. "We love you, too."

"She argue too much?" Seth asked when Robbie turned off the phone.

"Nah. Just bein' Mama. She's cool." Robbie leaned over the table and gave the cook a kiss. "Dinner's good, babe."

Seth shrugged and tried to hide a grin. "Thanks. Bein' on ranches, you eventually learn to cook relatively well."

Robbie nodded and started on his spare ribs. They were basted in tangy barbeque sauce, thick enough to warrant a wet towel instead of napkins. It was how you knew ribs were good: when they stuck to everything. He was sucking one finger after another, moaning at the unbelievable sauce, when he looked up to meet Seth's gaze. Those green eyes were riveted on him, specifically his mouth.

"Don't suppose you want dessert," Robbie teased, sliding a bare foot up Seth's calf.

"Not down here."

Oh, that look was fucking hot.

Seth stood, gathered their empty plates, and set them in the sink. Judging from the heat in that stare when he returned to the table, Robbie figured the dishes would wait. Seth reached down and hauled him up and into a kiss that shot fire along Robbie's spine. Breathless, Robbie stepped back and grabbed his cowboy's hand, dragging Seth out of the kitchen and up the stairs to their room.

The second the door was closed and locked, it was no-holds-barred. Robbie spun and pushed Seth back against the door, mouth crashing down for another hard kiss as he worked Seth's jeans open.

"Fucking want this," he breathed into Seth's mouth, inching his way beneath denim and cotton to get to skin. His fingertips skated across the tip of Seth's cock, spreading the pre-come over the crown.

Seth groaned, and his head fell back with a thud, fingers threading through Robbie's hair and tugging out the ponytail. "All yours."

Fuck yes, all his.

Robbie dropped to his knees and pulled that beautiful cock out. The head glistened with the clear drops, and he licked them away, moaning as the taste of Seth exploded on his tongue. Then he took Seth in slowly, inch by inch, until his nose was buried in curls. Seth's fingers tightened in his hair, his Texan fighting the urge to move. Robbie swallowed around the hard flesh in his mouth and worked Seth's jeans the rest of the way down. Grabbing Seth's hips, he let his cowboy know to move, to take what was needed.

"Oh, fuck." The words were groaned as Seth began moving, hips pumping slow and easy, that thick cock fucking Robbie's mouth. "Robbie."

"Mmm," Robbie hummed.

Seth's prick jerked on his tongue, flexing. Robbie ran his hands over Seth's tight ass, down to the creases where buttocks met thighs, then to the inside. His fingers skimmed across the tight hole there, pushing a little. Those muscled thighs spread for him. Robbie drew back, sucked his finger to wet it, before sliding it inside.

Seth jerked, thrust back into his mouth, and heat shot down Robbie's throat, thick and perfect. He swallowed every drop and licked Seth clean before sitting back on his heels, palm pressing against his jeans. Once Seth had his breath back, he stepped out of his jeans and kicked them to the side.

"Please, I need."

"What are you needin', babe?" Seth asked, big hands sliding under Robbie's arms to pull him to his feet. "Want me to suck you? Want to fuck me?"

Robbie didn't know what the fuck he wanted; he just knew he needed. "Anything."

Seth swatted his hand away. Within seconds, Robbie's jeans joined Seth's on the floor. Then Seth started working him backward, toward the bed, tugging Robbie's shirt off as they went. Robbie barely had time to get Seth's T-shirt off as well before he was shoved back, that fine Texas body following. Legs spreading automatically, Robbie's body made up his mind for him.

"Fuck me?"

Without a word, Seth reached for the bedside table and the lube sitting there. A squirt of gel, and then those big fingers were pushing inside, taking Robbie's breath away. He opened his legs as much as possible, bracketing Seth between them, hips rocking.

"Seth, please."

Seth withdrew his fingers and wasted no time in sinking his cock in to replace them. Robbie gripped Seth's shoulders.

"Love you," Seth whispered.

Beyond words, Robbie could only nod, body going out of control as heat built up quickly along his spine. "Now," he gasped, eyes rolling. "Fuck me."

His hands were caught, pinned to the pillow above his head, and then Seth gave him exactly what he'd asked for. Their sounds were muffled by a hard kiss, Seth's hips slamming into him, over and over, thick cock pushing past his gland with every thrust. Sparks ignited behind Robbie's eyes, and he jerked and bucked, heat spraying between them. Seth was right behind him, one, two quick, deep thrusts, and then filling him.

It took several more minutes before the world returned to normal. Robbie groaned as Seth pulled out slowly. Then he turned and curled up against his cowboy, hands petting the firm belly.

"So you think you can live with this?"

"You fucking kidding me?" Robbie kissed the smooth skin just to the right of Seth's right nipple. "We'll be lucky to see anything but the bedroom."

Seth's arms went around him, holding Robbie close. "Mmm...sounds like a plan."

Robbie nodded, eyes closing slowly. Sounded like a damned fine plan to him, too.

Part Three: December, 2006
Chapter Twelve

"Oh, Robbie! It's perfect!"

Robbie laughed and stood. After a moment, he cocked his head to the side, then dabbed a touch of white paint to the baby panda's eye before turning around. "Thanks. You like it?"

"Yes!" Kristy went up to the wall in front of him and reached out, but she stopped before touching it. "Is it dry yet?"

"Parts of it." He set the paintbrush in the glass of cloudy, gray turpentine and wiped his hands on the paint-covered rag draped over the back of the chair. "You seen Seth lately?"

"Um, think he ran to the store," Kristy said, gingerly running her fingertips over the baby giraffe's head. "Said something about chili for dinner."

Robbie's stomach picked that moment to rumble loud and clear. Seth's chili was positively to die for—thick and spicy as hell. Just then, the front door opened and closed, and his cowboy's deep humming resounded through the house to a somewhat out-of-tune Hank Williams Jr. song. Robbie shook his head, and Kristy chuckled.

"Believe me." Robbie grinned. "That mouth is much better at other things."

"Like...?" Seth asked from the nursery doorway. That long, beautiful body was encased in black cotton and faded blue denim. Green eyes teased Robbie from under the brim of a black Stetson.

"Oh, Lord. Y'all are hopeless." Kristy just rolled her eyes, laughing as she left the room.

"Hey, babe."

"Hi, yourself." Seth started toward him, almost stalking.

"You look like you're..." Robbie's words trailed off as Seth tugged him close.

Grinning against Robbie's lips, Seth whispered, "Like what?"

Robbie simply gave up on talking and took a kiss, humming happily when those strong arms wrapped tight around him. Seth smelled like chili powder and cayenne pepper. Painting forgotten, Robbie moved lower, nuzzling Seth's neck, drawing in the sharp spices and the scent of Seth himself—aftershave and the slightest hint of soap, flavored with a little touch of sweat and pure, one-hundred percent Texan male. Seth hissed as Robbie sucked up a mark, teeth scraping just a little.

Robbie finally stepped back, forcing himself to relinquish his hold on the man. "Okay. Anymore, and we'll never get anything done."

Seth chuckled. "No kidding. The nursery looks good. You're an awesome artist."

Robbie smiled. "Thanks. It's been a while."

"C'mon, babe," Seth said as he patted Robbie's right hip. "I've got chili to make."

Robbie hummed, his belly all for that five-alarm chili. "I need a cigarette, been painting for a while now without a break."

Before Robbie could walk away, Seth caught him for another kiss, keeping it nice and slow. Robbie's stomach growled, though, putting an end to the leisurely exploration.

"Cig. Chili. Texan. In that order."

Seth chuckled and headed out of the nursery. Giving that tight cowboy butt a good smack, Robbie left Seth to the chili-making and went for his cigarettes. Attention half on the news Kristy was watching, Robbie flipped the top of the pack open. He glanced down for a second to shake a cigarette out, but he didn't see anything beyond the silver ring taped to the inside of the top.

The sound from the TV disappeared, and Robbie's throat went dry. The need for nicotine dulled as he carefully removed the tape holding the ring in place. Setting the pack to the side, he stared at the ring, trying desperately to swallow the sudden lump in his throat.

An ivy vine wound around the silver band in a Celtic style, and the living room light sparkled off the polished surface as he turned it slowly. That's when he saw it, etched along the inside of the band:

Will you marry me?

The entire world faded away as Robbie turned around to see Seth standing in the kitchen doorway, smiling. Robbie could only nod, not trusting himself to even open his mouth. He didn't have a chance to say anything anyway, finding himself locked in a deep kiss, Seth stealing his soul just as surely as the man stole his breath.

"When did you do this?" he asked as Seth rested their foreheads together.

"Picked it up while I was out. I ordered the ring a month ago, had it made and engraved." Seth smiled, those green eyes staring right into Robbie. "Thank you," Seth whispered.

"For what?"

"For saying 'yes.'"

Robbie smiled and moved his hands up Seth's back, mapping the muscles beneath the shirt, loving the strength and heat he found there. "Where're we gonna do it?"

"Thought maybe we could check around. I doubt your Mama's preacher is interested in conducting a holy union."

"True."

Robbie lifted his head and just studied Seth's face for several minutes. He never intended to fall in love when he opened up to that first kiss so many months ago. He touched Seth's lips, tracing them lightly with a fingertip. A kiss was pressed to his finger, Seth smiling behind it.

"Love you," Seth mouthed, eyes never leaving Robbie's.

"Love you, too." Robbie dropped his hand to Seth's waist and leaned in for another kiss. "So much."

Chapter Thirteen

The next morning, Robbie pulled up into Mama's driveway and stared at the house for a minute. "You ready for this?"

"Absolutely."

"She's gonna flip. You realize that, don't you?"

Seth just chuckled. "Isn't that what the mother of the bride is supposed to do?" The man was out of the truck before Robbie could smack him.

"Oh. You are so in for it, Cowboy," Robbie growled as he got out. Seth stayed on the other side of the truck, grinning like hell. "Get your ass into the house."

Walking around the front of the truck, Seth smirked. "Promises, promises."

"Kiss my ass."

"Gladly."

Robbie's lewd response fizzled before he had a chance to say it when Mama opened the front door. "Hi, Mama," he called out, plastering on a not-so-innocent smile.

Mama eyed them both, stood to the side, and shook her head as she let them in the house. "What are you two up to?"

Once inside, Robbie looked at Seth, then Mama. Then he held up his left hand. Mama's eyes widened, and her mouth dropped open.

"Is that...?"

"Yep. He asked me yesterday."

Mama squealed and threw her arms around Robbie's neck. "Oh, baby!"

Robbie laughed and hugged her, grinning at Seth over Mama's shoulder. "Believe me, it was a surprise to me, too."

"Seth, come here." Mama beamed a wide smile up at Seth as she tugged him into what became a three-way hug. "I always wondered if y'all'd do it. Oh, I'm so happy."

Seth winked at him. "I was gonna wait 'til his birthday, but I couldn't wait that long."

"Well, I, for one, am glad that you didn't wait. Now, what're y'all thinking about for a ceremony?"

"Oh, Lord." Robbie rolled his eyes. "Here she goes."

"Hush, you." Mama let them go and went over to the kitchen table. She rummaged through her purse and came up with a small, battered notepad and a pen. Flipping it open to a blank page, she sat down and looked up at them. "Well? We got a wedding to plan, boys. Grab a couple of Cokes out of the fridge, and let's make some preliminary notes."

"She always like this?" Seth asked, eyes teasing as he got them both drinks.

"You watch it, mister," Mama warned, waving the pen at Seth as he sat down. "Else the grooms get pretty, dainty white bows and lots of lacy frills on the cake."

"Seth. Zip it."

Seth snorted, pressed his lips together, and made a zipping gesture over them.

"Good." Mama nodded. "Now, let's start with the guest list."

Robbie dropped down onto Seth's lap, and his cowboy grunted. "We don't want anything extravagant, Mama. Just a nice, little thing for friends and family."

Mama started writing, nodding her approval. "We can do that. I'll need a list of folks y'all want to invite—family and friends."

Robbie snaked an arm around to rub Seth's back. "We'll take care of it, Mama." He'd have to tell her, at some point, about Seth's dad.

The phone rang before Mama could really get started. She got up and answered it, wandering into the living room, leaving Robbie a little time to nuzzle. Seth's arms went around him, tight, holding on. Robbie breathed in deep, pulling the musky scent of Seth's aftershave into his lungs.

Mama sat back down a few minutes later and turned off the phone. "Now, where were we?"

"We convinced you that we'd handle everything," Robbie said, giving Mama his best angelic smile.

Mama simply raised an eyebrow at him. "You honestly think I'm gonna fall for that puppy-dog look, Robert Sexton?"

Seth snorted, pressing his mouth to Robbie's shoulder to stifle the sound. Robbie popped him on the head.

"Smartass cowboy. No, Mama, but you can't blame a man for tryin'."

"Anyway..." Mama eyed them both. "What colors are y'all thinking about?"

"Hunter green and black probably."

"Lots of ivy," Seth added.

"Ivy? This isn't something a mother wants to know, is it?"

Robbie laughed. "No, Mama. You *really* don't wanna know."

"Lord, Lord," Mama muttered. "So, small ceremony, hunter green, and black. It's more of a start than I expected to get out of the two of you." She scribbled on the paper, shaking her head a little. "Suppose the question of grandkids would be met with hysterical laughter?"

A mouthful of Coke could burn like hell when it went down the wrong way. Robbie coughed and spluttered. "Mama!"

"What?" Mama looked up, the look in her eyes something between innocent and teasing. "There's always adoption, ya know."

Seth's head landed on Robbie's shoulder, and Robbie's mouth simply dropped open.

"That one might be a while in the making, Mama," Seth muttered, though it sounded like the man was about ready to die if he held back his laughter any longer.

"Y'all are both nuts," Robbie grumbled.

A smile from Mama and a poke to his ribs from Seth had him laughing with them, though. Lord, the two of them were insane, but he loved them more than anything else in the world.

"Well, I think this is a good enough start," Mama said. She set the pen down and pushed the pad away. "How's the house comin' along?"

"Going great," Robbie said. "I just finished painting the baby's room. Kristy loves it. We need to get the truck loaded up and drop the stuff off, though. Gotta get to Mack's. We've still got a little left to pick up from there."

"Okay, baby." Mama stood, and Robbie got off Seth's lap. "Y'all take care. Let me know if you need help decorating or anything."

Seth smiled and hugged her. "We will, Mama."

Robbie gave her a hug and a kiss. "Thanks, Mama. Love you."

"Love you, too. Both of you."

Robbie followed Seth into the living room, and they started carrying baby furniture and stuff out to the truck. It didn't take nearly as long as he'd thought it would, and twenty minutes later, they were back on the road toward home.

"Think she'll be okay by herself?"

"Yeah. Mama's strong." Robbie glanced over at Seth and grinned. "She knows where we live. She won't be a stranger."

"No more fucking in the living room, huh?"

"Not with Kristy around!" Robbie shuddered as he turned onto their road. "God, so don't wanna go there, man."

A hand slid up his thigh, and Robbie inadvertently pressed harder on the accelerator. Seth squeezed his leg just below his crotch.

"I'll make it up to you."

Robbie slowed down as they neared the house. "You'd fucking better, damn it. That about killed your chances of getting any."

Soon as the truck was off, Seth tugged him over and into a hard kiss full of promises. Robbie groaned and shifted, hips lifting to push against the hand rubbing the growing bulge in his jeans.

"Inside," Seth murmured. His fingers made maddening circles over Robbie's denim-encased balls. "Want you."

Robbie had never moved so fucking fast in his life. He was out of the truck and at the front door before Seth even closed the passenger side door. Kristy wasn't in the living room or kitchen as they walked in, so Robbie headed straight for their bedroom, figuring she was napping. Last thing they needed was a sleepy-eyed woman walking in on them when he had his ass up in the air.

Seth caught him just as he stepped into their room. "Get naked."

Robbie tugged his shirt over his head before starting on his jeans. He kicked his shoes off, and then shoved the jeans down. Soon as he stepped out of them, Seth turned him around and bent him over. Hands braced on the bed, Robbie let his head fall forward, his breath catching as his underwear was slowly peeled off.

"Seth..."

"Don't move."

Something about being in this position—hands on the bed, bent over, ass up—made Robbie feel so fucking vulnerable...and needy as hell. He heard Seth open the bedside table drawer, and then close it. A moment later, two slick fingers circled his asshole.

"Seth, please," he whispered, hips grinding a little. "Stop teasing, damn it."

Seth chuckled and kissed the small of his back. Then Seth pushed both fingers deep, dragging a rough moan from him. "God, so hot."

Robbie would've answered, but nothing came out except sounds that didn't quite resemble words. He rocked back onto Seth's fingers, biting hard on his bottom lip when Seth curled them forward. Sparks bolted along Robbie's spine as those fingers teased and pressed, stroking his gland. Just when he thought he couldn't handle anymore, they were gone, and Seth was filling him, hands on his hips as his cowboy's cock stretched him open.

Balancing himself on one hand, Robbie grabbed his prick with the other. "Don't stop."

Seth rotated his hips, grinding against Robbie's ass. His cowboy's fingers dug into Robbie's skin as Seth tugged him back into every thrust.

Robbie threw his head back, shouting Seth's name as he shot onto the bed, entire body shuddering. Seth grunted and jerked him back hard, and Robbie moaned as the prick inside him swelled, pumping him full of heat.

"Goddamn, darlin'." Seth eased out, and Robbie collapsed face-first onto the bed, not giving a damn about the mess.

"Hell, yes. Oh, hell, yes."

Seth followed him down. "We still gotta go to Mack's."

"I know, I know," Robbie mumbled into the bed. He turned his head to the side and peered up at Seth. "This requires movement, doesn't it?"

"Afraid so."

Sighing, Robbie somehow managed to roll over. Out of habit, he draped his arm over his stomach, then immediately grimaced. "Oh, damn. I'm a mess."

"Actually, you and the bed are," Seth said. "Don't move."

"Last time you said that, I got my ass fucked."

"Smart ass it is, too.

Seth got up and went into the bathroom. He came back a few minutes later with a damp washcloth. He wiped Robbie's stomach, and then moved up to give him a slow, easy kiss as the washcloth moved lower. Robbie spread his legs, and Seth cleaned the rest of him.

"You realize if you keep doing that, we aren't gonna get anywhere," Robbie murmured.

One finger teased his hole. "Uh-huh." Then it slid in, the way still slick with semen.

"Oh, fuck..." Robbie moaned. He draped his right leg over Seth's hip as one finger became two. "Seth."

Seth's kisses moved downward, over Robbie's jaw, then to his neck. "Wanna feel you come. Just like this."

"Not sure I can...oh, God..."

Sparks shot up Robbie's spine as Seth's fingertips circled his gland. Robbie wrapped his hand around his cock and started stroking slow, Seth matching the rhythm with the thrust of his fingers. Robbie gasped, hips lifting, rocking as he jerked off, Seth driving him closer to the edge.

"Seth. Fuck..."

Seth pushed a third finger in and spread all three apart.

Robbie arched, heat spraying on his stomach, ass clamping tight.

"Now we can go," Seth muttered as he withdrew his fingers.

Robbie couldn't begin to form a coherent thought, much less think about driving anywhere. "You're driving."

Seth kissed Robbie's shoulder and rolled over. Motivating a body to move after not one but two mind-blowing orgasms wasn't easy, but Robbie finally managed to sit up. Okay, score one for movement. He could do this. He could get out of bed. Feet on the floor: check. Sitting upright: check. Soft bed: check. Warm, muscular body: check. A hand on his back kept him from lying down again.

"Up."

Robbie grumbled. "Yeah, yeah." He gave Seth's right thigh a thump and stood. "That goes for you, too, ya know."

"Yep." Seth managed to get dressed before Robbie even made it to the bathroom. "See?"

"Shut up."

Seth's laughter followed Robbie into the bathroom.

Chapter Fourteen

When Robbie came back out, he was sorely tempted to slap that denim-covered ass while Seth bent over to pull his boots out from under the bed. By the time he stopped ogling, Robbie lost his chance as Seth straightened back up. Giving his cowboy the best angelic smile he could, Robbie sat down and put on his own boots.

"What?"

"Nothing. Ready?"

Seth cocked an eyebrow. "Yeah..."

"Think we can get everything in one trip?" Robbie asked as they started out to the truck.

"Don't see why not. Not a whole lot left."

"Cool."

They got the truck unloaded from the first trip, and just as Seth was climbing up into the truck to head to Mack's, Robbie glanced around. Then he let the man have it. The sound of his palm popping denim was loud. Seth jumped, and Robbie busted out laughing, half-doubling over. Before he could catch his breath, though, he found himself up against the truck, facing the hood, with a big, firm hand on his right ass cheek.

"Tempting," Seth whispered in his ear.

Robbie shuddered, his prick going from soft to interested again within seconds. Seth's hand made slow circles over Robbie's ass, and it took all Robbie had not to push back against it.

"Not out here. God, what if the fucking neighbors see?"

"Shoulda thought about that first."

Seth's hand left, and Robbie had only a brief moment to prepare himself before his cowboy's palm connected with his ass. The sting bolted straight through his body, making him whimper softly.

Robbie was beyond mortified, doing this shit outside where anyone could see, but fuck if that didn't just make his prick swell even more. Either he was going to die from embarrassment, or from too many orgasms in a short time.

"Just one for now," Seth said. He released Robbie and stepped to the side, gesturing to the truck cab. "In. We'll finish this later."

Turning slightly, Robbie shoved his hand down his jeans and adjusted his cock. Then he glared at Seth over his shoulder. "Fucking tease."

Seth grinned. "Now, Robbie," he said as he got into the truck. "You know I always deliver."

Yeah, that's what Robbie was afraid of.

He got in and buckled, then chuckled when Seth leaned over and kissed him. "You're gonna be the death of me, Seth Ellis."

"Nah, wanna keep you around for a while, babe."

A hand squeezed Robbie's prick before Seth sat back up and started the truck. Jesus, it was gonna be a long day, and Robbie could still feel Seth's hand on his butt.

The drive to Mack's went quick, though Robbie figured that was partly due to his mind being on other things he'd never thought he'd think about. He was never the type to get into shit like that, but, damn. Something about Seth doing that twisted Robbie's insides into knots—good ones. Before he knew it, they were pulling up in front of Mack's farmhouse.

"You there?"

Robbie shook his head to clear it. "Yeah, just zoned out a bit."

Jack met them just as they got out of the truck. "Y'all here just to grab shit, or can you help out a bit?"

"We're here for whatever's needin' to be done," Seth said.

"Gotta repair the barn side. Damn termites ate right through the wood. Not a huge section, but it's muddy as all hell."

"You go get your stuff, babe. I'll help Jack right quick."

Seth nodded and tipped his hat. "We'll meet back up inside."

Robbie followed Jack over to the barn, and they both studied the small but rotten section of wood. Of course, it had to be surrounded by the only patch of mud in the immediate area.

* * *

"Always said you were a good man."

Robbie looked up, water hose in hand from where he'd been washing the mud off his boots. Mack stood there, leaning with one shoulder against the barn side, arms crossed. The man looked older, but just as strong and rugged as Robbie remembered from his childhood.

"I had good teachers," Robbie said with a smile.

Mack nodded. "That you did. Y'all get everything moved?"

"Yeah." Robbie turned off the water and looped the green hose around in a circle on the ground. "You sure you can manage here without him?"

"I'm sure. Got Jack and Ty, and Jeremy's workin' out good. He said he might be able to find another hand or two for me as well."

"Cool." Robbie wiped the water off his hands and held one out to Mack. Mack gave it a firm shake. "Can't thank you enough, Mack."

"You did good, kid. You're a good artist, and I don't think you could've found a better man than Seth Ellis. When's the wedding?"

Robbie blinked. They hadn't told anyone.

Mack laughed. "Susan, bless her heart, can't keep somethin' like that a secret. I'm happy for ya both."

Shaking his head, Robbie chuckled. "We haven't set a firm date. Mama's gone into a frenzy, though, wanting to plan everything to the smallest detail."

Mack smirked. "You should've eloped."

"We're beginning to agree with you on that."

"Does Susan know about his dad?"

Robbie looked across the yard where Seth was walking down the porch steps. "Not yet," he said quietly. He glanced back up at Mack. "How'd you know?"

Mack flicked a bug off his arm. "When he first got here, I asked for next-of-kin, for emergencies. He told me there wasn't any. I knew something was up, didn't wanna nose around, though. We got to talkin' and drinkin' one night, and he told me. Said he felt like he was holding back a nasty secret from a friend."

Robbie nodded. "He tried calling his dad a few months ago."

"Some bad blood there. Supposed to love your kids no matter what."

Robbie grinned as Seth started toward them.

"Was tellin' Robbie here, y'all should've eloped."

Seth laughed and took off his hat, raking his fingers through his hair. "Yeah, she's havin' a field day, that's for sure."

"Well, she doesn't have any girls to torment, so..." Mack chuckled. "All right, you two. Get cleaned up and meet me in my office."

When Mack was out of earshot, Robbie glanced at Seth. "He's got something up his sleeve."

Seth nodded as he watched Mack walk away. "Only God knows what."

"Might as well see what's up." Robbie gestured back toward the farm house.

"Hard to believe I'm movin' in with someone."

Robbie studied Seth for a moment. "You're okay with it, right?"

Surely, Seth wasn't getting cold feet now.

"Oh, Lord, yes." Seth laughed and put an arm around Robbie's waist, tugging Robbie against him, their hips bumping as they walked. "Just been on my own so long that I hope I don't run you off is all."

"Not a snowball's chance in hell."

Robbie led the way to his uncle's office, and Mack looked up from where he sat behind his big, beat-up wooden desk.

"Come on in, boys," Mack said as he opened one of the desk drawers.

Seth sat in one of the leather chairs, and Robbie took the one beside him. Mack pulled a dark brown leather ledger out of the desk and put it in front of him. He was silent as he opened it. Robbie couldn't help but wonder what the man had in mind. Mack was always full of surprises. Always had been, really. Robbie remembered days as a boy when Mack would sneak him huge pieces of homemade rock candy, much to Mama's chagrin.

"I owe you both for this week's work," Mack said. He took a pen out of the green and yellow John Deere mug. "Plus, a little something extra."

Extra?

Robbie caught Seth's curious gaze and shrugged. A couple minutes later, Mack tore out a slip of paper from the ledger and handed it to Robbie. Robbie's eyes went wide. It was a check, but not just for the four hundred for the week. He couldn't quite stop staring at the grand total of $1,400.00.

Mack tore out the second check and handed it to Seth, who had much the same reaction Robbie did.

"It ain't much," Mack said as he closed the ledger, "but I hope it helps y'all a bit. Wish I could do more."

Seth managed to regain his senses first. "Damn. Thank you, Mack. It's..."

"Awesome," Robbie finished, eyes still a bit wide as he looked up at his uncle.

Mack just smiled.

Chapter Fifteen

"Fuck!"

"That bad?"

Robbie grunted what he hoped sounded like "yes" and tapped the spark plug. "Fucker is welded in there, I swear. Why can't they make this shit easy?"

"Because they've got deals going with the dealerships and garages," Kristy said, leaning against the side of the truck. Robbie glanced up at her. "I'm serious! Haven't you ever found it just a little fucked up that cars break down so easily? Or that it takes more brute force than any human being has to, say, get a spark plug out?"

Rolling his eyes, Robbie chuckled. "You got a point."

Tires squealed, and they both looked toward the end of the road. Ice started to creep through the pit of Robbie's stomach the second he saw Russ' car.

"Get inside. If he tries anything, call the cops."

Kristy was already inside by the time Russ pulled to a stop at the curb. Robbie wiped his hands with a rag and watched his brother start across the yard.

"What do you want?"

"Wanna talk to Kristy."

"Turn around, Russ." Robbie stepped in Russ' path. "She wants nothing to do with you."

"Outta my way," Russ growled.

"Fuck you. This is *my* house." Robbie heard the lock on the screen door click into place.

"Goddamn faggot!"

Kristy screamed a split second before Robbie heard the gunshot. It took another few seconds before the pain really registered, bringing him to his knees in shock. A minute later, Kristy was easing Robbie onto his back, ripping his shirt open, her tears wetting his face. What a fucking way to start a morning.

"Oh, shit, oh, fuck...Robbie?"

Robbie groaned and reached up to touch his shoulder, but Kristy grabbed his hand. "Where's Russ?"

"Gone. He took off like a bat outta hell. Looked shocked that he did it. Cops are on their way." Kristy was talking a mile a minute, and Robbie hissed when she pressed a wadded bit of material on his shoulder. "Called 'em when he wouldn't turn around. Was on the phone when he shot you. Oh, God, I'm so sorry, Robbie." More tears dripped onto his cheek.

"Hush," he grunted. "You know better." Sirens wailed, and he let out a ragged sigh. "Call Seth."

Kristy sniffled. "You gonna be okay?"

He nodded. Within minutes, paramedics swarmed him. A cop stood off to the side, and Kristy went over to talk with him.

* * *

The second he pulled up, Seth just knew something wasn't right. For starters, Robbie's truck was in the driveway with the hood up, and Robbie was nowhere in sight. Seth didn't get the truck turned off before Kristy came barreling out the front door. Bemused, he watched as she sort of half-ran, half-waddled around to the passenger's side door. Seth opened his mouth to ask what was up, but it only took one look at Kristy's face to stop him cold.

"What's wrong?"

Kristy's cheeks were streaked with tears, and her eyes, normally bright and happy, were puffy and red. "Huntsville Hospital," she panted as she managed to buckle up.

"Oh, fuck...you're not—"

"No! No, it's Robbie." Kristy sorta twisted a little, and Seth's blood ran cold. "Russ came by. They argued, Russ wouldn't leave. Robbie blocked him from coming into the house, and Russ shot—"

Seth didn't hear anything beyond those last few words. He backed up the truck and took off down their street, shoving the pickup through the gears, heart thundering, knuckles white as his grip on the steering wheel tightened.

"I tried to call your cell, but just got the voice mail."

Seth gritted his teeth. "Wasn't getting a damn signal," he ground out.

Kristy put her hand on his shoulder. "He'll be okay. Robbie's tough—always has been."

He nodded. "I know."

They hit Memorial Parkway before he really knew it, which wasn't so good considering he was the one driving. He kept the speedometer at sixty and tried to keep down the urge to weave through the traffic. For a Thursday at nearly five, it was getting a bit busy. Fridays were the worst, though. He wondered if Robbie found a good shop for lease, then realized he was only trying to keep his mind off the fact that his lover had been shot.

He took the exit for Governor's Drive and merged into the rush hour hospital traffic. By the time they reached the hospital, his palms were sweaty, and his knuckles hurt from gripping the wheel so tight. He pulled into the parking garage, grabbed a ticket, and wound up four levels before he found a space close to the elevators for Kristy.

"You need a wheelchair, hun?" he asked as he parked and turned off the truck.

"Nah, let's just get you inside and to your man. I'm fine." She gave him a reassuring smile that went a long way to easing the tension inside him.

Seth gave her a nod and got out. Kristy joined him, and they headed for the elevators. As they waited for it to reach their level, he rocked back on his boot heels, hands shoved into his pockets. He noticed a couple of young women out of the corner of his eye, both of them staring at him like they'd never seen a man before. They couldn't have been more than twenty. Seth just shook his head.

The elevator dinged, and the doors slid open. He waited to the side as a family of four exited, then he stepped in, pressing the 'door open' button while Kristy, the two young women, and a man with two small children all managed to fit inside. Then he pushed the first-floor button and simply stared at the closed doors, willing the damn thing to hurry the hell up.

He barely stifled the sigh of relief when the elevator dinged at the first level. The doors opened, and he waited, holding down the button to keep the door open, until everyone else was out. Then he motioned to an elderly couple—a man pushing his wife in a wheelchair—to come in. He hopped out just before the doors shut again, tipping his hat at the couple seconds before their "thank you" faded behind the metal doors.

"Emergency, I'm assuming?"

"Don't know," Kristy said. "We'll stop by the information desk."

Seth followed her down the hall. They walked up to a long desk with several volunteers in dark blue blazers and gold nametags sitting behind it.

"Hi, we're looking for Mr. Robert Sexton," Kristy said. "He was brought in about an hour or so ago through Emergency."

"Just a minute," the man said. His fingers practically flew over the keyboard, and he nodded. "He's still in there." He stood and pointed down another hall. "Just go down that hall to the end and make a left. You'll find the nurse's station there, and they can tell you where he is."

"Thanks." Seth gave the man a nod, and he and Kristy made their way down the hall.

They had to wait several minutes before a nurse at the station was free to even look at them, much less answer questions. Finally, one turned to them and smiled.

"Can I help you?"

Seth sighed and stepped up to the desk, slipping off his hat. "Yes, ma'am, I hope so. We're here to see Robert Sexton. He was brought in about an hour ago."

"Are you family?"

"Well...yeah. He's my partner, ma'am."

Much to his surprise, the nurse smiled. "He's in room fourteen. I can only allow one person, though."

"You go," Kristy said. "He needs you. I'll be out here."

Seth gave her a kiss on the cheek and, hat in hand, followed the nurse. "Thank you, ma'am."

"Oh, no worries," she said as she swiped her badge on a scanner to open the double doors. "My cousin's been with his partner for ten years." She flashed Seth a bright smile. "Is the young lady family?"

"Might as well be. She's kind of a surrogate sister for me and Robbie at this point."

"How long y'all been together?"

The doors closed behind them, and Seth said, "'bout half a year. Planning a wedding. Well, a commitment ceremony, anyway."

"Oh, yeah? Congratulations!" She stopped in front of a curtained room. "He might be asleep. They've got him full of pain meds. If you need anything, my name is Susan."

Seth chuckled. "Easy to remember. It's my future mother-in-law's name."

"Cool." She pulled back the curtain a little and lowered her voice. "Just make yourself as comfortable as possible. You want a drink?"

"No, but thank you."

She smiled and nodded before turning and heading back to the doorway.

Seth stepped into the small room and pulled the curtain closed. Robbie wore the usual hospital gown, but Seth could see a bandage taped over and around his left shoulder. He pulled a chair up to the bed and sat down, taking Robbie's left hand in both of his. An IV was in the top of Robbie's other hand, and several wires disappeared under his gown. He didn't look too bad, save for the bandage. No bruises, no cuts. But, damn, just the sight of that bandage made Seth's throat feel like it wanted to close up on him. The wound was high up, but still on his vital left side.

The sounds of the emergency room just on the other side of the curtain didn't help to ease Seth's nerves any. It only reminded him of where they were. They should've been sitting at Mama's table, listening to her rattle on about only God knew what kinds of wedding decorations that neither of them knew the first thing about.

A tap on the wall snapped Seth out of his thoughts, and the curtain slid open a little. A doctor walked in and pulled the curtain to once more.

"Hi, I'm Dr. Hayworth," he said, extending a hand.

"Seth Ellis. Nice to meet you."

Dr. Hayworth nodded. "Are you together?"

Seth nodded. "Yes, sir."

The doctor just smiled, nodded, and set his folder down. "He seems to be doing okay." He put his stethoscope on and slipped the end under Robbie's gown, pressing it here and there, listening a few seconds each time. "Sounds good."

"What about his shoulder?"

Draping the stethoscope around his neck again, Dr. Hayworth picked up the folder and jotted something down. "The bullet went right through, completely missing bone, nerves, and major blood vessels. He's extremely lucky. May I ask what happened?"

"All I know is that I got home, and his sister-in-law came out to tell me his brother shot him. Have the police been in yet to talk to him?"

"Yes. I think they said they'll be back if they hear anything regarding his brother."

Seth sighed and rubbed his thumb over Robbie's knuckles. "How long you think he'll need to stay here?"

"Well, I'd like to keep him through tomorrow. I think he'll be good to go by Saturday, provided there aren't any complications. His shoulder will be sore for a few days, but about two weeks, and he should have full use back."

"Thank you."

The doctor checked the IV where it went into Robbie's hand. "No problem. If you need anything, just buzz a nurse or ask for me."

"Thanks."

Chapter Sixteen

Fuck.

Every damn thing hurt, but mostly his shoulder.

Robbie tried to open his eyes, but the bright light overhead threatened to burn his eyeballs out of their sockets.

"Too bright?" The light dimmed.

He knew that voice. Despite feeling like total shit, Robbie smiled. "Hey, baby." Only then did he realize Seth's hands were around his own. He tried to squeeze, but it didn't quite work. His arm was sore, though not quite bad enough for more pain meds. He hated being doped up like this.

"Hey there, yourself." Seth smoothed a hand over Robbie's forehead, brushing his hair out of the way. "How ya feelin', darlin'?"

"Like I've been shot."

Damn, that laugh was like the chorus of angels. Seth kissed him, lips just barely brushing Robbie's before Seth pulled back. Oh, hell, no. Robbie groaned and managed to open his eyes enough to give his cowboy a pitiful attempt at a glare. Seth laughed again and then those lips were back, moist this time, Seth's tongue pushing slowly in. Robbie hummed and gave as good as he got.

"Better?" Seth whispered.

"Much." Robbie tried to move his right arm and groaned. "Fuck, that shit hurts worse than the damn gunshot."

"Tetanus?"

"Yeah. The doc been in?"

"Yep. Said you'll be here through tomorrow."

"So much for shop hunting," Robbie grumbled.

Seth squeezed Robbie's left hand gently. "Have any luck?"

Fuck, these beds sucked a big one, and not in the good way. Robbie twisted and shifted as much as the wires, IV, and his shoulder would allow. "Not really. A few places for lease, but not what I'm looking for."

A knock sounded on the outer wall just as Seth opened his mouth to say something.

"Mr. Sexton?" a nurse asked.

"Yeah. Come on in, we're just talkin'," Robbie said.

The nurse smiled and drew back the curtain. "Your room is ready, so we're gonna get you up there and settled in for the night."

"Cool." Robbie looked around Seth, toward the sink counter. "Hey, babe. Can you grab my clothes and cigs?"

"Sure." Seth picked up the bundle and glanced at the nurse. "You need help movin' him, ma'am?"

"Oh, no," she said as she unlocked the brakes on the bed. "If you want, you can head up there. It's Room 433."

Seth set his hat back on his head and bent down to kiss Robbie. "I'll head up there and talk the nurse in charge into letting me stay the night."

"You sure you're up to sleeping here?"

"Absolutely."

"Thanks, babe. I'll see you in a few."

The moment Seth was gone, the nurse whistled low. "Why are all the hot ones gay?"

Robbie laughed as they started down the busy hallway. "I think I just got lucky is all."

"I'll say. He a real cowboy? Or just dress the part?" She turned a corner, and they lost sight of Seth.

"Texas-born and bred," Robbie said. He swore he heard the nurse sigh. "But I'm pretty sure there are others where he came from," he added. He tilted his head back and winked. Okay, so there was no one on earth like Seth Ellis, but the cowboy was his. All his.

The nurse wheeled him into one of the service elevators, and soon they were heading up to the fourth floor. When the doors slid open again, they went left toward the patient rooms. Seth was standing at the nurse's station just as they rolled past it. Robbie couldn't help but notice that ninety percent of the nurses were preoccupied scoping out his lover's ass in those tight-as-sin Wranglers. Hell, he sure couldn't blame them.

They stopped at Room 433, and, with surprising finesse, the nurse got Robbie's bed into the room without any trouble. She pushed the bed into place and locked the brakes. Then she hung his IV bag on a pole. Seth came in right about then, followed by another nurse.

"Hi, I'm Cary Ann, and I'll be your nurse until about seven tonight."

Robbie shook her outstretched hand. "Hi. Robbie Sexton."

The other nurse left, and Cary Ann set her folder on the rolling table. Then she pulled the thermometer out of its read-out box. Slipping a cover on it, she stuck it under Robbie's tongue. A few minutes later, it beeped, and she removed it. Seth sat down on the chair by the bed and set his hat on top of Robbie's clothes.

"Looks good. How's your shoulder?"

Robbie moved his shoulders a little. "Achy but not too bad. Other arm hurts more thanks to the tetanus shot."

"Sounds about right." Cary Ann laughed. "If you need anything, just buzz the desk. You're allowed to drink."

"Oh, good. Pepsi?" Robbie looked at Seth. "Want anything, babe?"

"Pepsi's fine, thanks," Seth said with a nod and a smile to the nurse.

"I'll be back in a few minutes then."

When she left, Seth stood and came over to the bed. "How're you *really* feeling?"

"Am I that transparent?"

"No. I just know you."

Rolling his eyes, Robbie let his head fall back onto the pillow. "I hate hospitals."

Seth rubbed a hand along Robbie's right leg. "Hey, look at it this way: it's only for one day."

"Thank the gods."

Cary Ann returned with their drinks. "There you go. Just buzz if you need anything."

"Thanks." Robbie pushed the button on the bedrail to raise the head up. "Ah, much better."

When the nurse left, Seth popped the cans open and poured Pepsi into the two small cups full of ice. Then he handed one to Robbie.

"I want to go home," Robbie grumbled before taking a sip.

"I know, babe. Believe me, hanging out at Huntsville Hospital is not my idea of a fun night."

Just before Robbie could say another word, someone knocked on his room door. He groaned and let his head fall back against the pillow. "Come in."

"Robbie?" Oh, shit. Mama'd been crying. Still was, actually. She walked over and kissed his forehead. "Oh, baby. Why'd he do it?"

He had a million answers to that, but Robbie dutifully kept them to himself. "He tried to get to Kristy, Mama."

Mama sniffled. "Where'd we go wrong?"

"Mama, look at me. Please?" When she pulled back, Robbie looked up into her eyes as they filled with fresh tears. "Mama, you and Dad didn't do anything wrong. Russ is an angry man—he always has been."

Another knock sounded, and Robbie just barely stifled the growl. Fuck! This whole shit was getting to be ridiculous. His eyes widened when he saw two men, one a uniformed cop, standing in the doorway.

"Mr. Robert Sexton?"

"Yes?" Robbie answered.

"I'm Detective Cantrell. We need to speak with you a moment, please."

"Want me to leave?" Seth asked.

"Detective, this is Seth Ellis, my partner, and my mother, Susan Sexton. I'd prefer they both be present."

The detective nodded, and the other officer closed the door, giving them all some privacy. Detective Cantrell glanced at Mama. Getting the hint, Seth stood and pulled up the chair, silently coaxing Mama to sit down. A bitter knot began forming in Robbie's gut. This wasn't going to be good.

"We tried to take Russ Sexton quietly, but he refused to pull over. He lost control of his car and hit a telephone pole. The coroner said your brother probably never felt a thing."

Mama cried out, and Seth dropped to his knees, holding her tight. Despite the hell Russ had put him through, Robbie felt something tighten and shatter inside. He closed his eyes slowly, and it took a moment before he could form any words. Mama's wails broke his heart. No parent should ever hear about their child's death.

"I'm very sorry," the detective said. "We need someone to come identify the body."

Mama let out another broken cry, twisting everything inside Robbie. He just waved the detective away, still unable to open his eyes. If he did, he'd cry. No matter how much he despised Russ, the man had still been his brother—adopted or not.

"We'll wait outside."

When he heard the door open and close again, Robbie finally looked over at Mama and Seth. For the first time in his life, he simply felt empty. Dad's death had been hard, but at least they'd seen that one coming.

Seth kissed Mama's head and murmured something to her. She nodded, and they stood up. He helped her to the small bathroom near the door, and Mama went inside, pulling the door to, but not completely shut. Seth returned to the bed.

All he had to do was put his arms around Robbie's neck.

Robbie broke down, no longer able to hold back the tears threatening to rip him apart.

Chapter Seventeen

The next day passed like any other. The sun poured in through the blinds on the window, and the world continued to turn as if nothing had happened.

Robbie turned off the TV and dropped the remote onto the bed. His arms were sore—the right from a needle, and the left from a gunshot. It was almost surreal when he thought about it. He couldn't really remember a time when he and Russ had really gotten along, but he never wished the man dead. A soft knock on the door pulled him out of his thoughts.

"Come in."

The man wearing a "chaplain" name tag closed the door and smiled. "Good morning, Mr. Sexton. I'm Joseph Rutledge."

As he shook the chaplain's outstretched hand, Robbie figured the man couldn't be much older than himself. "Nice to meet you. Just call me Robbie."

Joseph nodded. "Feel free to call me Joseph. You didn't specifically request a visit, but you didn't express any disinterest in it."

"It's okay. You're welcome to sit down." When the chaplain settled into the chair, Robbie continued. "I guess I should tell you now that I'm not Christian. I was raised Baptist, but I've been pagan for more years than I can really remember at this point."

"That isn't a problem," Joseph said. "We see people from many faiths. We aren't here to judge or change anyone. We are simply here to listen and talk, to pray and help heal the soul so the body can heal."

For the first time since waking up at six that morning, Robbie smiled. "Thank you."

"How are you feeling?"

"I'm assuming you don't mean physically."

Joseph chuckled softly. "I mean in all aspects of being."

Robbie rested his head back on the pillow and closed his eyes. It took a few seconds before he could form the jumble of thoughts into some cohesive order. "I don't know how much you know about why I'm here."

"I know you were shot in the shoulder by your brother, and that he passed away yesterday."

"That's pretty much it," Robbie said. "My parents adopted Russ when I was ten. He was two months old. I think the age gap had a lot to do with the rift between us, but my being gay didn't help either, especially when Russ was the first to find out after catching me with a friend. After that, he hated me. Honestly, I wasn't exactly fond of him either."

"So you think your sexual orientation was the start of the troubles with him?"

"I'm guessing so, though when Russ found out he was adopted, he blamed my parents. Hated my father for it and was ambivalent toward Mama."

"I see. How did they take it?"

"Dad passed away a few months ago," Robbie said.

"I'm sorry."

"Thanks. We knew it was coming. He was a smoker. I've thought about quitting, but right now, I just don't have the courage or the willpower."

"How did you and your father get along?"

Robbie shrugged. "I loved him, and I know he loved me, but we weren't really close. He would've flipped if he'd known I was gay. I wouldn't say he was a homophobe, but he wouldn't have liked it one bit."

"What about your mother?"

Now that made Robbie smile. He opened his eyes and stared up at the ceiling. "I adore her. Not sure how else to put it. She's been so accepting of me since Russ outed me before Dad's funeral. She's even flown into wedding frenzy since Seth and I announced our engagement."

"Congratulations."

"Thanks." Robbie looked at the chaplain. "It's Seth, though, who's kept me sane through everything. I don't know what I'd do without him."

"How long have you been together?"

"Since the beginning of the summer, 'round June, I think. Seems like it's been longer, though."

"How are you feeling regarding your brother?"

Robbie bit his lip and looked out the window to Governor's Drive below. "I don't know," he said quietly. "When Dad died, it was hard, but like I said, we knew it was coming. But Russ..." He shook his head. "It was a shock more than anything. I couldn't stand him, but I never wished the man dead."

Another knock came from the door, and it opened a moment later.

"Oh. Sorry," Seth said. "I can come back later."

"No. Wait." Robbie held out his hand. "Joseph, I'd like you to meet my partner, Seth Ellis. Seth, this is Joseph Rutledge, one of the hospital chaplains."

"Nice to meet you," Seth said with a smile as he shook the chaplain's hand.

"Nice to meet you as well." Joseph stood and clasped his hands behind his back. "Robbie, if you'd like to speak again, just call down to the chapel. If I'm not in there, they'll find me."

"Thanks. And thanks for listening."

Joseph smiled and, unless Robbie had lost his mind, gave him a tiny wink. "My pleasure. Anything for family."

As the chaplain walked away, Robbie noticed a silver ring on his right ring finger. To anyone else, the rainbow-colored gems were decorative, but to Robbie, they were proof the chaplain was more understanding than most.

"You okay?" Seth asked once the door was shut. He sat down on the bed beside Robbie and rubbed Robbie's thigh.

"Yeah." Robbie smiled up at him. "I think I am, babe. You find what you were looking for?"

"Yep. Parking pass has been validated, so we don't have to pay a dime. Any word from the doctor?"

"Just waiting on the release papers," Robbie said. "I need to go home, Seth. I hate hospitals, and I don't like sleeping without you."

"Soon, darlin.'"

* * *

By the time they got home, Robbie was itching to do something, anything, so long as it didn't involve sitting in a bed. Kristy was quieter than usual, but she gave him a big hug when he and Seth walked in the door. Thankful that he just had a bandage as opposed to a sling, Robbie held her, rubbing Kristy's back slowly with his other hand.

"You okay, hun?"

Kristy nodded, though she didn't pull away, just kept her face buried in his shirt. "Yeah. Yeah. Just..." She drew in a shaky breath. "It's just hard, ya know?"

"I know." Robbie kissed her hair. "But we can get through this."

Lifting her head, Kristy smiled up at him, despite her red, puffy eyes. "I know we will."

"Hey, baby, you hungry?" Seth asked from the kitchen doorway.

"A little. Wanna get changed into something more..." Robbie looked down at the sweatpants. "...normal."

"Normal?" Kristy laughed and sniffled. "Honey, there ain't nothin' normal about you. It's why we love you."

"Brat." She ducked before Robbie could pop her on the head. "Anyway...yes, I want my damn jeans."

He threw Seth a glance before heading down the hallway. Just as he reached their bedroom door, one arm snaked around his waist and tugged Robbie back against a blessedly hard body. Robbie opened the door and walked in, pulling Seth with him.

"Get naked, Cowboy." He turned and shoved his sweatpants to the floor. I wanna ride you. Can't be on bottom right now, but, damn it, I can sure as fuck ride."

"Hell, yeah."

Seth got undressed and stretched out on the bed. One hand pumped his cock with slow, lazy strokes, while Seth reached up for the lube with the other. He got slick, and Robbie crawled over him. Robbie moaned as he sank down onto that beautiful prick. Nothing compared to this—the sensation of Seth filling him, stretching him.

"Robbie." Seth's fingers dug into Robbie's hips, and his cowboy started moving, slow and easy.

"God, yes," Robbie whispered. He closed his eyes and just rode—hips rocking back and forth, the pleasure building deep inside him with every stroke. His own prick was hard as steel.

Seth drew his legs up, changing the angle. The strokes quickened, and Robbie wrapped his fingers around his cock, jerking in time to Seth's movements. "That's it."

Robbie cried out, coming so strong, it brought tears to his eyes. He was barely aware of Seth's moan and the cock inside him swelling. Breathless and shaky, Robbie fell forward. Wrapped in Seth's arms, he broke down, stress and anger and tension melting out of him in a rush.

"Love you, Robbie."

Robbie just nodded and held on tighter. The past few days had shaken up his entire world, but this man—this one anchor in his life—put him back onto solid ground.

Part Four: February, 2007
Chapter Eighteen

"Is this really necessary?" Robbie groaned when Mama stopped at yet another florist. This was the third one—today. "Mama, it's a small ceremony. Nothing fancy, remember?"

"Nonsense," Mama said as she got out of the car. She bent and peered in the window. "Well, you comin'?"

Robbie sighed and unbuckled. "Yeah."

By the time he got out and closed the car door, Mama was already walking into the shop. He shook his head and went inside. He could beg, bribe, and plead his case until the end of time, but once Mama set her mind to something, there was no stopping the woman. Robbie couldn't really blame her, though. With Russ gone, Mama didn't have anyone else to dote on—well, except Kristy, and that was a whole other kind of doting. Since Russ' death, Mama had thrown herself headlong into baby and wedding planning. It made her happy, though, and that's all that mattered.

"There he is. Robbie, this is Carol Withers. You went to school with her...niece, was it?"

"Yeah, Kat was in a few of my classes," Robbie said, offering his hand to his former art teacher.

Carol smiled, the look sympathetic. "Hi, Robbie. Actually, Mrs. Sexton, Robbie was one of my best art students."

"Oh, that's right!"

"How is Kat, anyway?" Robbie asked.

"She's fine," Carol said. "Mrs. Sexton, if you like, I can show you a few arrangement books of work I've done."

"That would be wonderful, thank you."

Giving Robbie a wink, Carol got Mama settled at the round table off to the side of the counter. With Mama's attention diverted, Carol inclined her head toward the door and tapped two fingers to her lips. Robbie gratefully followed her outside. The door hadn't even closed before Carol lit up.

"You looked like you needed a break," she said around the cigarette while offering her lighter.

Robbie tapped out a smoke from his pack and lit it, inhaling deeply. "Oh, yeah. She's a whirlwind."

"So how are you doin', kiddo? How'd Baltimore go?"

"Doing good, got a good man, thinkin' about my own shop."

Carol nodded and blew out a plume of smoke. "Guess you finally came out to your mama, then?"

"Yeah, was kinda forced to thanks to Russ. And right before Dad's funeral, too." Robbie caught Carol's grimace when he glanced back in the window at Mama.

"I heard about Russ," Carol said. "Not gonna give you the 'I'm so sorry' crap since I know you better than that, but how are you feeling?"

Robbie shrugged and leaned back against the brick wall, staring at the Memorial Parkway overpass in the distance. "Better than I thought, to be honest. Hell, you know how things were between me and Russ."

"I do. Wish it could've been different, but I'm just glad you're doing okay. So what about this new man?"

"His name's Seth Ellis. Transplanted from Texas. I met him at Mack's, and we haven't stopped since."

"Cowboy, huh?" Carol grinned. "Nice. Guess it's a stupid question to ask if you love him."

Robbie laughed. "As cheesy as it sounds, I never believed in love at first sight until I met him."

"Cool." Carol stubbed out her cigarette. "Your mama's probably wonderin' what happened to us."

Robbie put his out as well. "If she asks, I didn't smoke. Ever since Dad was diagnosed with cancer, she's been militantly anti-tobacco."

"Can't say I blame her when it comes to her kids." Carol opened the shop door.

Mama turned another page, and Robbie groaned as he neared the table.

"Thought we were sticking to ivy."

"I've been looking at ivy, too," Mama said. "Look." She spun the book around so Robbie could see.

Okay, so it wasn't quite as bad as he'd expected. The arrangement was simple but elegant—ivy curled around a white trellis. He could live with that. Hell, it was actually kinda nice. Robbie nodded.

"I think that'll work. It's nice but not frilly."

Mama beamed. "Great!"

"Any idea where the ceremony will be?" Carol asked.

"Umm..." Robbie gave her a sheepish grin while Mama shook her head. "Not yet."

"Robbie's been rather busy lately," Mama added. "Lookin' to open his own shop."

"Find any places yet?"

"Found a few, but nothing that struck me as the right place, ya know?"

Carol nodded. "I know the feeling. Definitely good luck, though. If I hear anything, I'll let ya know."

"Thanks."

"Oh, I need to get going," Mama said when she glanced at her watch. "I have an appointment at the salon." She stood and shook Carol's hand. "We'll be in touch now that he's finally found something he likes in the floral department."

Carol laughed and patted Robbie's shoulder as they headed outside. "No problem. You've got my card. Just call, and we'll set things up once you have a date."

"See you later, Carol," Robbie said, waving before he got into the car.

"Well, three shops, and you survived." Mama chuckled and started the car once they both buckled up.

"Yeah, yeah. Oh, what're we doin' for Kristy's birthday tomorrow night?"

"Hmm..." Mama pursed her lips and pulled out onto Triana Boulevard. "Was thinkin' Jazz Factory, downtown. That okay with you guys?"

"Are you kidding? You're asking me if steak is okay?"

Mama laughed. "Good point, and they do have the most wonderful ribeye with those garlic mashed potatoes. Jazz Factory it is, then."

* * *

"So how'd it go?"

Robbie dropped into the recliner and let his head fall back against the seat. "After three shops, we ended up at my old art teacher's place. We found a good ivy trellis thing there."

Seth chuckled and knelt down, arms resting on Robbie's knees. "You look like you've seen enough flowers to last you a lifetime, babe."

"I have."

"Wanna go grab a shower?" Seth's hands sort of migrated a few inches up Robbie's thighs, those green eyes going hot.

"Make me forget about flowers?"

"Damn right." Seth bent forward and exhaled on Robbie's jeans, breath hot through the denim.

"Jesus," Robbie hissed, hands going immediately to Seth's hair, fingers threading through soft brown. "Seth..."

Seth tugged at Robbie's jeans, popping the button. "Shower. I'll fuck you into oblivion."

Robbie didn't need any more encouragement than that. The promise of the beautiful cock was more than enough to get Robbie moving. He didn't need to look to know Seth was right behind him. He felt the man's stare, Seth's gaze hot as hell and burning through his jeans. Seth muscled him into the bathroom and locked the door. Strong hands caught Robbie's hips, tugging him back against that hard body. Robbie chuckled and shot Seth a smirk over his left shoulder.

"Kinda difficult to get the shower going if I can't move."

Seth sort of walked them over to the tub and put a hand on Robbie's back, bending him forward. "By all means..."

The hard ridge of his cowboy's cock pressed against Robbie's ass, and he groaned. "Seth. Fuck." He couldn't help but push back when Seth rotated his hips a little.

"That's the idea," Seth murmured, shoving Robbie's jeans down.

Once the water was going good and hot, Robbie stripped the rest of the way and stepped into the shower. He watched Seth undress and crooked his finger, beckoning his own personal sun god to join him. Seth got in, and Robbie filled his hands with hot, wet skin.

"Jesus, you're fucking gorgeous." Robbie trailed his fingers down Seth's chest, carding them through the sun-lightened hair to the tanned skin beneath.

Seth tunneled his hands in Robbie's hair and cupped his head, reeling Robbie in for a slow, deep kiss that curled his toes. Aware of nothing but those lips, that tongue, Robbie didn't realize they'd even moved until warm water poured down over them. Seth ran his hands down Robbie's sides and around to grip his ass, hauling him up against Seth's muscled body. Their pricks rubbed and slid, water providing just the right amount of slick.

Robbie moaned into Seth's mouth, a little bit breathless. "Seth, please..." His ass cheeks were parted, and Seth tapped his hole with one finger. Robbie rose up on his tiptoes, every nerve focused on that one spot.

"Trust me?" Seth asked as he snagged the lube from the shower caddy and slicked his cock.

"Fuck yes."

Seth pressed Robbie up against the tiled shower wall. "Put your legs around me." When Robbie did, Seth reached down and lined up, cockhead rubbing Robbie's hole. Seth pushed in deep.

Robbie moaned, the sound muffled when Seth's mouth covered his. He tightened his arms around Seth's neck, hips rocking, riding every slow, deep thrust his cowboy made. Heat built slowly, need and pleasure coiling low and spreading through his body.

"Don't stop."

"Never."

Seth shifted his angle, and his cock grazed Robbie's gland. Robbie jerked, breathless as Seth kept moving, muscular thighs putting force behind every stroke. Eyes wide, Robbie gasped, bucking in Seth's arms as spunk splashed between them.

"Oh, yeah..." Seth grunted and crushed their mouths together, tongue pushing inside as his cock swelled, pumping Robbie full of heat.

Panting and shaking, still clinging onto Seth, Robbie let his head fall back against the shower wall, breaking the kiss. "Damn, babe."

Seth chuckled softly and brushed a kiss to the hollow of Robbie's throat. "Water's getting cold."

"Uh-huh. Bed?"

"Bed."

Chapter Nineteen

Bright and early at eight, Robbie knocked on the office door of the minister of the Unitarian Universalist Church of Huntsville. A moment later, the door opened, and Joseph smiled at them as he stepped to the side.

"Good morning," he said, ushering Robbie and Seth into the small office.

"Mornin', Joseph." Holding his hat in one hand, Seth shook the minister's outstretched hand with the other.

Joseph shook both their hands before turning to Robbie. "How are you feeling?"

Robbie smiled. "Feeling great, actually. Thanks for meeting us today."

"I'm happy to. Please make yourselves comfortable."

Hand on Seth's back, Robbie guided his lover to the couch along one wall. Joseph took the armchair a few feet away, facing them, forgoing the formality of the desk. They spent the next two hours talking about the ceremony itself, how they met, and what they each hoped for in the future—together and individually. By ten o'clock, Robbie felt they had a good plan in place.

Joseph sat back and linked his fingers before him. "Do you have any questions for me?" The light caught the rainbow of stones on his ring, setting off brilliant sparks of color.

"Being, well, pagan in my beliefs, I'm afraid I don't know much about the Unitarian Church," Robbie said. "I assume they are accepting of gays and lesbians?"

"Yes." Joseph absently toyed with his ring. "We are the only ones, now that MCC is gone, who openly and fully accept the LGBT community. Others might accept gays and lesbians, but it's rare that they allow us to hold positions within the ministry."

"I take it you're out then?" Robbie asked.

Joseph nodded. "I am. My partner Dan is the church's secretary."

"Nice to find family around here," Seth said.

"It is indeed," Joseph answered with a smile just as the phone rang. "Excuse me, please." He got up and went to the desk to answer the phone.

"You hungry?"

Robbie's stomach growled, and he laughed. "Yeah. Any ideas on lunch?"

"How about we grab something to go and bring it back up here?"

"Oh, that sounds good. Burger King?"

"Burger King it is," Seth said.

"I apologize, gentlemen," Joseph said, hanging up the phone. "I'm afraid I'm going to have to cut our meeting short."

"Oh, that's fine." Robbie stood, and Seth did as well. "We were just talking about lunch. You have our cell phone numbers, right?"

"Yes, and here's my card should you need me." Joseph handed Robbie a white business card with a picture of a flaming chalice. "Thank you for agreeing to meet so early."

"Not a problem." Seth held out his hand, and Joseph shook it. "Take care, and we'll be in touch."

"You, too."

Once outside, Robbie slipped his hand into Seth's back pocket as they headed toward the parking lot. "God, I love it up here. One of these days, I want a house in the mountains. Our own place, far away from the rest of the world."

"Sounds like a dream worth working for, darlin'." Seth unlocked the doors and went around to the driver's side. Soon as they were buckled, he started the truck and pulled out of the parking lot. He turned left onto Governor's Drive and headed down the mountain.

Twenty minutes later, lunch in hand, they started back up Monte Sano, bypassing the church this time. Although the little bit of frost that covered the ground in the morning was now gone, the air was still cool enough to need a coat. Mid-February, and still no snow. It figured.

"You know, we still haven't settled on a place for the actual ceremony."

"I know," Robbie said. "Mama suggested Big Spring Park downtown." He shrugged. "Not secluded enough if you ask me."

Seth made the turn into the state park entrance and headed toward the picnic area. "Well, what about the mountain?"

Robbie watched the woods out his window and mulled things over. "It's a possibility. Any particular place in mind?"

They pulled into a parking space, and Seth turned off the truck. "Maybe. Come on."

Laughing, Robbie got out and handed Seth their drinks. Carrying the bag of food, he followed Seth to the picnic pavilion. When Seth found a table, Robbie sat and waited for his cowboy to elaborate.

Instead of explaining, though, Seth just sat across from Robbie and started on his burger. Robbie shook his head while he ate. After they finished and threw their trash away, Seth took Robbie's hand and led him only God knew where.

"You're up to something."

Seth chuckled. "What makes you say that?"

"I know you, Cowboy." Robbie gave the man a wary look out of the corner of his eye.

"Have I ever led you astray?"

Robbie opened his mouth to respond, but any words died before they left his lips. "Oh, wow. I haven't been here in ages."

What had once been a Depression-era tavern was now a shell of stone. Robbie touched the wall reverently, memories of climbing the steps, of peering through long-forgotten windows, rushing back to him. Monte Sano Tavern had been built by the Civilian Conservation Corps in 1937 and had been a popular place in the thirties and forties before fire gutted it in 1947. Although there had been talk here and there of rebuilding it, a part of Robbie hoped they wouldn't.

"I remember coming here and playing, pretending this was a fort. You know they've talked about rebuilding?"

Seth walked over and sat on the steps leading up to the opening of what used to be the front door. "Yep. I first came up here a few days ago. Got curious about it, read the sign, and checked it out online. It's really special to you, isn't it?"

Robbie nodded, ascended the steps, and jumped down onto the ground in what he assumed was the main room. "Yeah, it is. Just something about it, ya know? So much history in these stones." He heard Seth land just behind him, and then arms circled his waist.

"So, why not here then?"

"Really?"

Seth shrugged, chin resting on Robbie's left shoulder. "Why not? It's beautiful, even if it's chilly up here."

Smiling, Robbie leaned his head back against Seth and took in the stone ruins that had once been one of his favorite places to play as a kid. "Yeah, babe. I want to get married right here."

* * *

They got back home around two in the afternoon, and Seth left shortly thereafter to help out at Mack's in Athens. Robbie cruised slowly down Bob Wallace Avenue, keeping an eye open for any small shops for lease. Choices were slim, and he finally pulled into yet another shopping center parking lot.

"This is ridiculous. There's gotta be something out there suitable."

Just as he started to get out of the truck, his cell phone rang. He dug it out of his jeans pocket and flipped it open.

He smiled when he saw Seth's name pop up. "Hey, babe. What's up?"

"Jeremy said Dragon's Ink just closed about two months ago. Have you gone down Drake yet?"

"No. I will now, though. God, that'd be perfect." He somehow managed to get buckled again while holding the cell to his ear. "Thanks, babe. And tell Jeremy thanks for me."

"Will do. Love you. See you around five."

"Love you, too. Five works. We're taking Kristy to Jazz Factory."

"Okay. Bye."

"Bye, babe." Robbie hit 'end' before starting the truck again.

Drake Avenue was just one street down, and in no time flat, he pulled up in front of what used to be Dragon's Ink Tattoos. He grabbed his cell and dialed the number of the realtor on the window.

"Thank for you calling Evans Realty. Can I help you?"

"Yes, my name is Robert Sexton. I'm calling about the storefront at 1423-C Drake Avenue, used to be Dragon's Ink Tattoos. Is there someone who could let me in so I can check things out? I'm interested in leasing."

"Let me check."

Robbie got out and waited on hold while peering through one of the big front windows. Once his eyes adjusted to the dark inside, he saw the front counter, then the hall leading back. He thought he could see at least four doorless rooms, two on each side. There was another door at the very end of the hall. Oh, man. It'd be perfect.

"Hello, Mr. Sexton. Jim Graham here."

"Hello, Mr. Graham," Robbie said.

"You're interested in the old Dragon's Ink storefront, I understand."

"Yes. I am. I just moved back down here in the summer after a three-year stint in Baltimore. I'm renewing my license down here."

"Wonderful. I don't have any appointments until five-thirty, so I'd be happy to show you the place. I can be there in about ten minutes."

"Great. Thanks."

"Thank you."

Robbie hung up and grinned. "Fuckin' A. Please be affordable."

Ten minutes later, a steel-blue Ford Taurus pulled up beside his truck. A middle-aged man in a dark gray suit got out, leather briefcase in hand.

"Mr. Sexton?"

"Hi. Call me Robbie." Robbie held out his hand, and the man shook it.

"Pleased to meet you." Jim pulled a set of keys from his pocket and unlocked the glass door of the storefront. "So you're a tattoo artist?" he asked as he held the door open.

Robbie stepped inside, nodding. "Yep. Used to work at Seven Nations here in town, and then headed up to Baltimore because I needed a break from Alabama. Back home now and ready to open up my own shop."

"Well, as you can see, this location is perfect for it. You're welcome to look around. If you have any questions, please feel free to ask."

"Thanks."

Robbie walked down the hall and peered into each room. They were small, but typical for a tattoo shop. A wooden bench with a leather seat lined one wall in each one, and the opposite wall held a long mirror above a built-in counter top. Cabinets ran the length of the counter at the bottom. There were no chairs, but Robbie figured he could probably get some relatively cheap if he checked with Seven Nations.

The back door led into a store room with a good niche for a desk. Yep, this was perfect. Now for the fun part. He closed the door and headed back out to the front.

"Well, looks great," he said, shoving his heads into his pockets. "How much is the lease a month?"

"One thousand and seven hundred dollars a month with a one-year lease. There's a security deposit of six-fifty, which is refundable at the end of the lease if you don't renew. The shop is eight hundred square feet total."

Robbie nodded and thought it over. This was definitely doable. He'd need a loan from the bank for equipment, but his credit was good enough for that. "I need to talk it over with my partner, but it's what I'm looking for."

"Excellent! Here's my card," Jim said, handing Robbie a white business card. "Just let me know, and I'll draw up the lease agreement."

"Thank you."

They went back outside, and Robbie shook the man's hand. Soon as he got in the truck, he called Seth's cell.

"Hey, babe," Seth said. "Any luck?"

"Actually, yeah. The old Dragon's Ink place is seventeen hundred a month with a year lease and a six-fifty deposit. I'll need to get a loan from the bank for equipment, but you think we can swing it?"

"Sure. Don't see why not. What about staff?"

"Well, I was gonna ask you about that. Hold on." Robbie set the phone down and buckled up, then picked the cell back up. "How would you like to work the desk?"

"You think the income will be enough?"

"I think so. Hell, might as well be going in as business partners on this anyway."

"True."

"And I'll sell artwork on the side since Seven Nations wants it."

"Cool. I think we can do it. If need be, I can work for you part-time and find something else part-time to supplement."

Robbie popped open the glove compartment and got his cigarettes. After lighting one up, he blew the smoke out the window. "Okay, that works. I'm headin' back home. Need a shower before tonight."

"I'll be there around four looks like. I'll need a shower, too, and Mack says he's good."

"Okay. I'll see you then. Love you."

"Love you, too, babe."

Robbie hung up and started the truck. Hell, yes. Finally. His own damn place.

Chapter Twenty

It was kinda nice to have the place to himself. Robbie tossed his keys on the table by the couch and headed for the bedroom, tugging his shirt off as he went. He threw it into the hamper and opened the closet. Jeez, what the hell was he gonna wear? He hadn't been to Jazz Factory in a while. He remembered they were a bit more on the fine dining side than, say, Red Lobster, but they weren't quite suit-and-tie. He finally decided on a pair of black dress pants—his only pair, actually—and a nice dress shirt. He tried to avoid ties altogether. Damn things felt like nooses.

He set his clothes out on the bed and went into the bathroom to start the shower. After a quick study in the mirror, he figured he could avoid shaving. Facial hair never seemed to grow fast for him, thank God. Now, Seth, on the other hand. Robbie shivered at the thought. Just something about Seth with a five-o'clock shadow was enough to make him ache.

"Robbie?"

"In the bathroom," he called.

Kristy stepped into the doorway, and Robbie was glad he hadn't taken his jeans off yet. "Where we goin'? Mama won't tell me." She crossed her arms and pouted. On anyone else, it would have been annoying, but on her, it was cute in a kid-sister kind of way.

"Not a damn clue," Robbie said. He gave her a nonchalant shrug. He got a slap on the arm for it. "Hey!"

"Liar." Kristy tilted her head, nose in the air. If she hadn't been trying like hell to hide the grin threatening to break out, Robbie would've thought she was really pissed.

"You really think I'm gonna tell you?"

"Not a snowball's chance in hell, huh?"

"Nope." Robbie winked and started to close the door. "Gotta shower. Seth will be home shortly."

"Asshole."

"Brat."

He laughed when she stuck her tongue out, then he shut the door. When the shower was nice and hot, he stripped off the rest of his clothes and stepped in, pulling the curtain closed. God, he needed this. He tipped his head back and slicked his hair off his face, eyes closed as the heat from the water seeped into his muscles. Meeting with Joseph, lunch on the mountain—those had been fine. It was the driving all over Huntsville that was tiring as hell.

"Now there's a sight to come home to."

Robbie nearly jumped out of damn skin. "Jesus, Seth."

Seth chuckled.

"Join me?"

"If I do that," Seth said, "we'll be late for dinner. I'll jump in after you."

Seth winked and left Robbie to finish up. When done, Robbie stepped out, and Seth took over.

It was a miracle, but they somehow managed to get it all done without fucking. Towel around his waist, Seth stood at the sink and opened the cabinet. Robbie grabbed Seth's wrist before Seth could get the shaving cream out.

"Don't."

"Why not? Lord, I'm gettin' scruffy."

"Please? I'm curious."

Seth smiled slowly, meeting Robbie's gaze in the mirror. "I see."

Dear God, Robbie felt that stare right through him. It was a fucking wonder Seth never got into porn with a look like that. "Wanna see you with a little stubble. Not that you really need it to be sexy as sin."

Seth laughed and set his razor down. "As you wish."

Robbie turned and left before they ended up on the damn bathroom floor. Or over the counter. Or, hell, anywhere. He got dressed as quickly as possible, forcing his mind on mundane stuff to will away the hard-on. It didn't help a bit when Seth paraded that naked, sexy ass right in front of him, though. And damned if Seth didn't bend right the hell over, thighs apart, to dig for only God knew what in the bottom drawer of the dresser.

"You're cruel."

"I'm just looking for something to wear."

"Sure. And I'm not standing here, debating on making us late for our reservations in favor of shoving my cock up your ass."

Seth winked at him over one shoulder. "What better dessert, eh?"

Robbie sighed. "It's gonna be a long night."

* * *

Robbie grumbled and tugged the blanket over his head. "Sun's too fucking bright."

A deep chuckle sounded beside him. "And this is different from usual, how?"

"Shut up."

Seth laughed and pulled the blanket down until Robbie stared up into green eyes. "I could suggest a way to block the light..."

One eyebrow raised, Robbie eyed the man dubiously. "And that would be?"

Seth leaned down, lips just barely touching Robbie's. His cock, hard as stone, rubbed against Robbie's left thigh. "Suck my cock."

Robbie licked his lips. Then he sat up and shoved the man onto his back. Seth spread his legs, and Robbie settled between them on his stomach. He buried his face in the curls and breathed deep.

"Sweet fuck, you smell good."

Seth's fingers ran through Robbie's hair, letting it fall forward to brush those muscular thighs and the washboard stomach. "Smell like sex."

"Smell like us, babe." Robbie licked Seth's balls and watched them draw up toward the man's body. Seth groaned, legs parting a little more. Robbie licked again. And again.

"Having fun down there?" Seth chuckled.

"Mmm..." Robbie tongued just beneath Seth's right ball and sucked it gently into his mouth. The growl he got was pure heat, and it vibrated through Seth and into him.

"Robbie."

Robbie hummed, and his cowboy's fingers tightened, hands fisting in his hair. He released the right and rolled the left on his tongue before drawing it slowly into his mouth, moaning around it. Pressure on the back of his head pushed Robbie's face up against Seth, and his own cock throbbed under him, aching. He let go and, despite the hold Seth had on him, pulled back and looked up.

"Suck it."

Robbie wrapped his fingers around the base of Seth's cock and circled the crown with his tongue. Moving up, he licked away the drops of pre-come, then sealed his lips around the head and sucked. Seth's hips jerked upward, but Robbie held the man down with his other hand on Seth's hip, determined to play.

"Robbie," Seth growled.

Chuckling around the hard flesh in his mouth, Robbie sank down ever-so-slowly, knowing damn well he'd pay for it later. But, fuck, it was worth it. Seth let out a long, deep groan, and Robbie finally let the man move. He reached up and flicked Seth's nipple ring, and Seth's hips snapped up, thrusting that thick cock down Robbie's throat.

"Oh, shit." Seth started fucking Robbie's mouth with quick strokes, hands in Robbie's hair to hold him still.

Robbie moaned and sucked, and, sweet fuck, he needed to come so damn bad. He let Seth take over, let the man use his mouth. Just the sheer thought of it had Robbie humping the bed, cock swelling. With a particularly hard thrust, Seth shot, cock pumping salty heat right down Robbie's throat. That was all it took. Robbie's cry was muffled as he came, heat spreading over the bed under him.

Breathless, jaw aching but in a good way, he pulled off, licking Seth clean before he dropped his head to his cowboy's thigh. "Holy fucking shit."

Seth laughed and patted his head. "Now that's my idea of waking up."

"Not moving. Ever again." Robbie got a thump on the head for that one.

"I know I'm high in those essential proteins, but you think we could get something to eat?"

He snorted and slapped Seth's thigh. "Asshole."

"Yours. And I'm hungry. Want pancakes?"

Robbie really didn't wanna get up, but his stomach had other ideas. Food. Good. Seth's pancakes. "Okay, you talked me into it."

"Cool. Lemme jump in the shower right quick, and then it's pancakes. Wanna join me?"

"Nah. I'm gonna call Jim Graham and tell him we'll take the shop."

"Okay."

Robbie sat up so Seth could get out of bed, then he scooted up and grabbed the cordless on the nightstand. "Hey, babe. Where's Jim's business card?"

"On the dresser by your wallet," Seth said before starting the shower.

Crawling across the bed, Robbie stood and found the card under his wallet. After dialing the number, he sat down and pulled on his lounge pants.

"Jim Graham here."

"Hi, this is Robbie Sexton, the one interested in the Dragon's Ink place for lease."

"Oh, hi there!"

"We want it. Talked it over with my partner, and we decided it fits what I'm looking for in a shop."

"Excellent. I'll get the lease agreement drawn up today. I just need your address, full name, numbers, and your partner's information if she's going to be on the lease."

"He, actually, and, yes, I'd like him to be. He'll be working at least part-time for me."

Jim didn't skip a beat, which was nice. "I apologize. Need to remember to ask. Not the first time."

"Hey, ya never really know," Robbie said. "Okay, you ready for our address and numbers?"

"Shoot."

Robbie spent the next ten minutes giving Jim their names, address, cell phone numbers, email addresses, and only God knew what else. By the time he got off the phone, Seth was walking into the kitchen in nothing but a pair of jeans. Damn. Robbie set the phone down and followed. He slipped both arms around the man's waist, leaning close to nip Seth's neck.

"Mmm...everything cool?"

"Yep. He's drawing up the lease today."

Seth nodded and patted Robbie's hands. "Gotta let me go if you want pancakes, babe."

"Yeah, yeah." Robbie kissed the tanned shoulder and let Seth do his thing. "Need to get my license renewed, too."

"Should be okay, right?"

"Oh, yeah." Robbie got the coffee started, then sat down at the table. "Just need to brush up on medical-type stuff."

"Kristy still asleep?"

"No, I think I heard her moving around in her room. Mama said the doc was gonna watch Kristy close, though."

"Everything all right?" Seth turned and gave him a worried look.

"Yeah, just this being Kristy's first baby, and, what with the abuse she's been through, he just wants to make sure things progress smoothly."

"Baby's due any day now, isn't he?"

"Yep. Gonna be interesting having a baby in the house."

Seth chuckled and started mixing up the batter. "Oh, yeah."

"Robbie!"

Robbie was out of his chair in seconds, Seth right on his heels. He opened Kristy's door and knew immediately what was going on. "Seth, call the doc!"

"Done."

"Oh, shit," Kristy gasped, panting and holding her belly. "Oh, fuck. Robbie."

"Shh, we're good, honey, we're good. Where's your suitcase?"

Kristy panted a bit and pointed to the closet. "Blue one."

"Seth's calling the doctor. I'm going to take your suitcase out to my truck. Okay? Seth will still be inside if you need someone."

"Okay. Hurry."

"Will do." Robbie went to the closet and grabbed the blue suitcase and left the room. "Seth!"

"Doc is gonna meet us there. You take her. I'll call Mama and pick her up. We'll meet you at the hospital."

"Thanks, babe." Robbie gave Seth a quick kiss and hurried out the door. Just as he tossed the suitcase in the back, Seth came to the doorway, walking Kristy down the steps. Robbie opened the passenger's side door and helped Kristy into the cab.

"Drive safe. We'll be there soon."

Robbie got in, buckled, and started the truck. "How ya doin', hun?" he asked, glancing at Kristy before backing out.

"They're about three and a half minutes apart," Kristy said. She wasn't panting anymore, but her voice still held a touch of pain. "He said first-time births can take a few hours, to several hours."

"Did you decide on a name?"

"Christian Robert Conner."

Robbie smiled over at her. "Really?"

Kristy nodded. "You don't mind your nephew having your name for a middle name, do you?"

"You kiddin'? Hell, no!"

Kristy laughed, and then groaned, her head falling back. "Okay. No more laughing. Just drive."

"Driving."

Robbie got them there quickly but safely. He pulled up at the front door of the Huntsville Hospital for Women and Children building. He got out, and the attendant brought over a wheelchair. Together, they got Kristy into it.

"You gonna be okay while I go park?"

"Yeah, I'm good. What about Mama?"

"Seth's bringin' her. You just take it easy, okay?"

Kristy nodded, and the attendant pushed her inside. Robbie got back into the truck just as the cell rang. He flipped it open and pulled around toward the parking lot.

"Hey."

"Hi, baby!" Mama said, apparently using Seth's phone. "We're on our way. How's she doing?"

"She's good. She's inside, and I'm parking the truck."

"How far apart are the contractions?"

Robbie found a space and pulled in, then turned off the truck. "She said three and a half minutes. I'm thinkin' it's definitely time."

"Yeah, that close, I'd say so. Wanna talk to Seth?"

"Not while he's driving. Tell him I love him, and I love you, too."

"Okay, baby. Love you, and we'll be there shortly."

Chapter Twenty-One

The day flew by, or at least it seemed like it did. Kristy made Mama's year by requesting Mama to be with her during the delivery. Besides, it gave Mama something to focus on so she wasn't sitting in the waiting room and worrying.

"Thank God for nurses and their stash of playing cards," Seth said as he dealt out yet another hand of poker. As for how many games they'd played, Robbie lost count somewhere around twenty-two.

"No kidding." Robbie gathered up his cards and rearranged them. "What time is it?"

"Umm..." Seth tugged his cell phone out of his pocket, giving Robbie full view of at least half his cards.

Robbie bit back a grin and moved his two queens to the left with the two kings. When it came to playing against Seth, he wasn't above a little cheating. The man normally kicked his ass.

"It's almost seven-thirty," Seth said soon as his phone came back on.

"Wonder how Kristy's doin'. She's been back there practically all day."

"Mr. Sexton, Mr. Ellis?"

Robbie looked up at the young nurse beside them. "Yes? I'm Robbie Sexton."

"Hi, I'm Annie. Ms. Conner is doing very well, although she's tired. Are one of you the father?"

Seth laughed and shook his head. "Oh, no. We're the uncles."

Annie smiled. "Well, congratulations on your new nephew. Christian Robert came in at seven pounds and twelve ounces, and twenty-one inches long."

"Can we go back yet?" Robbie asked her as Seth packed up the cards.

"Sure. Ms. Conner is in her room now with Mrs. Sexton. She's on the fifth floor, room 523."

"Thanks."

They dropped the cards off at the information desk, and then started for the elevators. Joined by a young man and a little girl, they got in, and Seth pushed the button for the fifth floor.

"What floor?" he asked.

The man nodded toward the buttons. "Fifth. One of y'all a new daddy?"

"Uncles," Robbie said with a grin. Okay, whether he knew a damn thing about babies or not, he was still excited as hell about this one.

The elevator dinged, and the doors slid open. Robbie grabbed Seth's hand and practically tugged the man down the hall toward Kristy's room. The door was open, and Robbie peered inside. Kristy looked up and squealed.

"Robbie!"

"Hey there, kiddo!" Robbie let go of Seth and went to Kristy, giving her a tight hug. "How ya feelin'?"

"Oh, shut up. I can see right through you." She grinned and pointed over at Mama.

"Come and say hi to your new nephew," Mama said.

God, Robbie had never seen her so happy. Mama glowed almost as much as Kristy.

Robbie sat down, and Mama handed the wrapped bundle of wrinkles and pink skin over. "He's so tiny." The baby stared right up at him, blue eyes probably taking in far more than anyone could possibly imagine. "Hey there, baby boy. I'm Uncle Robbie. Wanna meet Uncle Seth?"

"Howdy," Seth said, crouching down beside Robbie's chair. He reached out, and a tiny hand, with the tiniest fingers Robbie had ever seen, grasped Seth's big index finger. "Wow. You got a grip, kid."

Robbie looked up at Kristy, who smiled at them. "What are you gonna call him?"

"Chris, I think. Don't wanna confuse everybody by callin' him Robbie."

"God, he's beautiful, Kristy," Robbie whispered.

"Thanks. I'm rather partial to him, too."

Seth laughed and finally managed to pry his finger loose. Chris, however, did not appreciate it. His mouth opened, and Robbie knew what was comin' before the kid started screaming. Seth held out his finger, and within seconds, it was in Chris' mouth, the baby more than content. Robbie just laughed.

"Playin' favorites already, huh?"

A nurse poked her head in the door. "Ms. Conner, I'm afraid visiting hours are over. You can have one person stay overnight if you like. The big chair opens into a bed."

"Mama, will you stay?" Kristy asked.

"Of course, baby." Mama got up, and Robbie handed Chris back to her. The baby looked like he was gonna start up again, but Mama smiled and tapped his nose. "Now you hush. Gonna hand you back to your mama so I can see my boys off." She put

Chris in Kristy's arms, then came back to hug Robbie and Seth. "You boys drive safe, okay?"

"We will, Mama. Get some sleep. Want us to bring anything tomorrow?"

"Nope. Brought my suitcase when Seth got me."

"Cool. Love you." Robbie kissed her cheek.

"Love you, too. Both of you."

Seth's hand in his, Robbie left the room. As usual, he couldn't help but notice the nurses checking Seth out, heads turning as they walked by the nurses' station. Robbie chuckled.

"What?"

"Fucking love having my own personal cowboy."

"Okay..."

"Nurses love you, babe. Hell, women in general love you."

Seth flashed him a wicked grin. "But I'm all yours."

"Oh, hell, yes."

Despite a slow elevator, three fussing kids, and traffic from hell, they finally made it home. Robbie barely had his keys on the table before Seth manhandled him toward the bedroom. When Robbie tried to pull his shirt off, Seth swatted his hands away and did it for him. Robbie chuckled and started on his jeans, only to have the same thing happen seconds after his shirt landed somewhere on the floor in the hall. This was their last night of peace before things got interesting with a baby in the house.

Seth turned him around and, as soon as Robbie was naked, shoved him back onto the bed. "Get yourself ready."

God, he loved when the man got all growly and pushy. Robbie rolled over and got the lube off the night stand and slicked two fingers. He snapped the tube closed and drew his legs up, watching Seth as his cowboy undressed.

"Gonna fuck me, Cowboy?" Robbie gasped as he pushed two fingers deep inside himself.

"Damn right." Seth's jeans and shirt hit the floor.

"Need your cock, Seth. So thick, stretching, filling." Two fingers joined his, and Robbie groaned, spreading his legs as much as possible. "Yeah. Oh, God, Seth, now."

Seth pulled their hands away and lined up. Hands on the backs of Robbie's thighs, he shoved Robbie's legs to his chest and thrust hard, driving his thick cock deep. Robbie shouted, sparks bursting through him, chased by a touch of pain. Goddamn.

"Want it slow and deep?" Seth pulled out slowly, and then rocked back in, grinding his hips against Robbie's ass.

Robbie could only nod. He gripped the backs of his knees and held his legs tight to his chest. His hips lifted, and the angle when Seth thrust back in was fucking perfect. Seth's cock stroked over Robbie's gland, sending shocks right up Robbie's spine. Seth kept it up—withdrawing slowly, then thrusting back in, pushing hard and driving his cock deep. Nothing else existed but his asshole and that cock, pumping in and out in an excruciating rhythm. The urge to come wasn't enough to make Robbie move. He just wanted Seth to keep going all damn night—filling him over and over.

"Oh, my God." It hit him out of nowhere. Robbie cried out, shaking uncontrollably, asshole clenching tight around Seth's prick while his own pumped a load of spunk on his chest.

Seth grunted and started fucking hard and fast. Then he slammed inside, cock swelling and filling Robbie right the hell up. Seth eased Robbie's legs down and kissed him. "Last night of quiet for a while."

Robbie nodded. "I know. Wanna order pizza? Watch a movie or ten?"

Chuckling, Seth pulled out and flopped over onto the bed. "Sounds good to me. You do the pizza ordering, and I'll do the movie. Anything in mind?"

"Hmm...action. How about Chronicles of Riddick?"

"Sounds damn good to me. Extra pepperoni and cheese?"

"Absolutely." Robbie leaned over and stole a kiss. "Meet ya in there."

Seth got up and went into the bathroom. A moment later, he tossed a slightly-damp towel to Robbie before putting on a pair of sweats.

Robbie wiped up and pulled on his cotton lounge pants, then found the phone hiding under a shirt on the dresser. He dialed the number for Domino's and headed for the kitchen.

"Thank you for calling Domino's. How can I help you?"

"Yes, I'd like to place an order for delivery."

"Go ahead."

"Two large pizzas, extra cheese and extra pepperoni on both." He opened the fridge and grimaced. "And two two-liter Cokes."

"Will that be all?"

"Yes."

"Your address?"

Robbie gave the guy their address, only half paying attention when Seth wandered past the kitchen door.

"We'll have that out to you in thirty minutes, Mr. Sexton."

"Thanks." Robbie hung up, grabbed the last two bottles of beer, and went into the living room. "Pizza's on the way." He tapped Seth's shoulder with one of the bottles.

"Thanks, babe. Have a seat."

Robbie sat down, feet on Seth's lap, and took a drink. "Gonna be interesting."

"Oh, yeah. We're gonna have to learn how to change diapers." Seth glanced over at him. "You realize that, right?"

"Don't remind me. At least Kristy's breastfeeding."

"They say it's the best thing, right?"

Robbie took another swallow and nodded. "Yep. She'll have to pump occasionally, though."

"Never thought I'd be having this conversation." Seth snorted and popped open his beer. "I like kids, but I'm definitely not the type to have them myself."

"What about a dog? I could live with a dog."

"Now dogs, I can handle. Want one?" Seth asked.

"Possibly. Well, maybe in a few months. I'd rather get a puppy, but training one while dealing with a baby would be a bitch."

Seth groaned. "Okay. Good point."

Epilogue: April 16, 2007

"You nervous?"

Robbie let out a slow breath. "Am I that obvious?"

Seth chuckled and wrapped his arms around Robbie, tugging him back against that solid body. "Believe me, babe—so am I. You gave the rings to Ty and Jack, right?"

"Yep." Robbie covered Seth's hands with one of his own.

They'd forgone music, opting for the sounds of nature instead. It had been a hard sell with Mama, but she eventually warmed up to it. Telling her about Seth's folks wasn't as bad as Robbie had thought, either. He hadn't been too surprised when she'd gotten angry at Seth's dad for every bit of it.

Robbie watched the small group of friends and family take their seats in the two rows of folding chairs set up to face the front of the tavern. The ivy-wound trellis stood in the center of what Robbie assumed had been the front porch of the tavern. Jack and Ty, decked out in their best Wranglers, dress shirts, boots, and hats, waited on either side of the trellis.

From his place under the trellis, Joseph raised his hands, book in the right. "Ladies and gentlemen. Friends and family. Thank you for joining us this afternoon in celebrating the union of two wonderful gentlemen."

That was their cue.

Robbie and Seth walked to the tavern side by side and up onto the porch to stand before Joseph.

"Robert Sexton, do you accept Seth Ellis as your partner in all things, to travel through life with you, to share in the joys and the sorrows, forsaking all others?"

Robbie smiled over at Seth. "I do."

"Seth Ellis, do you accept Robert Sexton as your partner in all things, to travel through life with you, to share in the joys and the sorrows, forsaking all others?"

Seth squeezed Robbie's hand in his. "I do."

"The rings?" Joseph held out the open book while Jack and Ty placed the rings in the middle. "Robbie and Seth have their own vows to share with one another. Robbie, please place the ring on Seth's finger."

Robbie picked up the ring and took Seth's left hand. With a deep breath, he slipped it on, and then looked up. It took a second to get around the lump in his throat. "Seth Ellis, you've been the rock I've leaned on, the listener I've needed. You've been a best friend and a beautiful lover. Now, I wish you to be my partner for the rest of our lives."

Seth smiled and gave Robbie's fingers a little squeeze.

"Seth, please place the ring on Robbie's finger."

Picking up the ring, Seth lifted Robbie's left hand and kissed his knuckles so softly that Robbie nearly crumbled right then and there. As Seth slipped on the ring, he said, "Robbie, being with you surpasses everything I have ever dreamed of. I can't imagine life without your smile, without your laughter, without your touch, without you. I love you."

Robbie wasn't even aware of the tear until Seth reached up and brushed it away with his thumb.

"May your lives be blessed," Joseph said, "and your years filled with happiness."

With a nod from Joseph, Seth pulled Robbie into a kiss that simply broke the barriers down. Robbie didn't give a damn who saw the tears. He just draped his arms around Seth's neck and kissed the man with everything he had.

* * *

"You really don't have to—" Robbie laughed and gave up when Seth lifted him and stepped through the doorway. Arms around the man's neck, Robbie just smirked. "You just had to be the big macho man, didn't you?"

"Darlin', I'm from Texas." Seth gave him a lewd grin. "Everything's big."

"Oh, don't I know it. You gonna show me just how big?"

"Damn right." Seth set him down and closed the front door. "Kristy and the baby are at Mama's, ya know."

"Uh-huh." Robbie started backing up toward the couch. "Dinner?"

"Dinner's good. Ain't cookin'. Neither are you."

"And I'm not letting you out of this house," Robbie said.

"Nope."

"Guess we're ordering in. Steak Out?"

"Yep." Seth grinned when Robbie misjudged and fell backward onto the couch. "Distracted much?"

"Can you blame me?" Robbie asked, propping himself up on his elbows. "You gonna order this time?"

"I can. You gonna get naked and find us a movie?"

Robbie knew damn well what movie he'd put on. "Yep." The Internet was such an awesome thing.

When Seth went into the kitchen, phone in hand, Robbie got up and ran back to the bedroom. He found the bag he'd hidden in the closet and pulled out the DVD, the new bottle of lube, and the double-ended dildo. He tore open the package, stripped, and hurried back to the couch. By the time Seth was done ordering dinner, Robbie had one end of the dildo lubed up.

"Dinner's on...holy fuck." The phone landed on the recliner, and Seth walked around to stare down at Robbie.

Robbie drew his legs up and parted them, rubbing the head of the dildo over his hole. "Bought 'em about two weeks ago." He nodded toward the DVD on the end of the couch. Then he pushed the dildo in, groaning as it stretched his hole open. "Oh, God..."

"You expect me to watch a porno when I got *this* to watch?" Seth put the DVD on the coffee table and knelt beside the couch. He leaned down and licked Robbie's lips before parting them with his tongue.

Moaning, Robbie opened up, pushing the dildo deeper as he sucked on Seth's tongue. Then he felt Seth's fingers tracing his hole where it stretched around the toy. Before he could pull the thing out, those fingers were sliding in. Robbie's eyes popped open, and Seth broke the kiss, gaze burning right through Robbie as his cowboy added a third finger.

"Fuck me."

"You gotta take this out first."

Robbie shook his head.

Seth's stare went white-hot, and he pulled his fingers out. He stood and undressed, then knelt again. "Turn this way." He helped Robbie turn until Robbie's ass was hanging off the couch, dildo still buried deep. "You sure you're up for this? It's gonna hurt, baby."

Robbie watched Seth lube up his cock and nodded. "Yeah. Please."

Seth rose up and rubbed the head of his cock along Robbie's hole, just under the dildo. "Just relax as much as possible."

He tried. Oh, fuck, he tried, but when Seth started pushing inside, stretching him wide open, Robbie's brain shorted out. His eyes rolled back, and it took all he had to hold onto the dildo instead of grabbing Seth and jerking the man against him.

"Seth..."

"So fucking tight, Robbie."

Seth went slowly, but Robbie wanted to get fucked. Now.

"F-fuck..." Robbie panted, lips dry, ass on fire, and cock so hard, it fucking hurt. "Oh, God...Seth..."

Seth's fingers dug into the backs of Robbie's legs as his hips pressed up against Robbie's ass.

"Move. Now. Seth!"

Robbie arched, body nearly coming off the motherfucking couch. Seth started pumping, cock sliding in and out alongside the dildo. Robbie shouted, coming so hard and fast, it brought tears to his eyes.

Seth slammed into him, and Robbie could only moan as the cock inside him swelled, filling him even more.

Breathless and sore as hell, Robbie melted into the couch. Seth pulled out slowly, and then eased the dildo out.

"Not moving. Ever."

Seth chuckled and leaned down, giving him a soft kiss. "Love you," he whispered.

"Love you, too. So fucking much."

"Oh, got you something. Get dressed."

"Huh?" Robbie blinked as Seth got up and put his pants back on. "What?"

"Just stay there and put your pants on. Got you a little wedding gift." Seth disappeared into the kitchen, and Robbie heard the back door open. What the hell?

Then he heard it. A fucking bark. Okay. Not a bark. A yip. Robbie barely got his damn pants on before an overgrown fur ball attacked him out of nowhere. He plucked white fur out of his mouth and laughed at the bright eyes staring up at him—one brown, one blue.

"Like him?" Seth asked, leaning over the back of the couch and scratching the Malamute puppy behind the ears.

"He's gorgeous!" Robbie tipped his head back for a kiss, but the squirming thing in his hands had other ideas and licked him right on the neck. He laughed into Seth's mouth.

"What's his name?"

"Ellis," Robbie said.

"Ellis? For a dog?"

"Why not?"

Seth grinned and shrugged. "We could always name him Sexton and call him Sex for short."

"That was bad. So fucking bad."

The dog barked, the sound shrill. Robbie looked at him, and the puppy tilted its head curiously, tail thumping Robbie's leg.

"You like Ellis?" He got a bark in response.

"All right, all right." Seth came around and sat down beside Robbie. Ellis pounced him. "Hey, boy. You gonna be a good guard dog? Take care of the baby?"

Ellis licked him.

"Hey now. No one licks my cowboy but me!"

Seth set the dog down when the doorbell rang. Ellis yipped and nearly tripped Seth up on the way back to the couch. "Okay, you heathen. Outside while we eat." He scooped up the dog and carried him outside.

"Thank you for the dog, babe. I've been so busy trying to get things ready to open up the shop that I totally forgot to get you a gift."

Seth sat down and turned Robbie's head, meeting him in a kiss. "Don't need one," he whispered. "I got you."

About the Author

Alter ego of Katherine Cook, Mychael focuses on gay erotic romance stories in many genres. She lives in the eastern US with her family.

Read more at https://mychaelblack.com/.

www.ingramcontent.com/pod-product-compliance
Lightning Source LLC
Chambersburg PA
CBHW071912220626
47052CB00002B/313